May you spend
a few happy hours in
Sunny Acres.
Naomi Williams
5/19/12

SUNNY ACRES

by

NAOMI WILLIAMS

This is my letter to the world....
Judge tenderly of me.

Emily Dickinson

Dedication

To my editor, Peggy Cheney, who has brought Sunny Acres *from its infancy to its maturity. Her sharp eyes have perused each page as her red pen encircled not only blank spaces and typos but also more serious errors such as inexact quotes and need of amplification in character and plot. Thanks, Peggy, my former student, my dear friend, and my Editor of* Sunny Acres. *This book belongs to both of us.*

Foreword

Although *Sunny Acres* is set in a fictional Lifecare Community, I have used very liberally the description of the Brandon Wilde complex where I live as an independent resident in Evans, Georgia. The book, however, is novelistic, because the characters and situations are fictional with the exception of those who gave permission to use their names and personal events. My intent is not to offend anyone but to present with humor and pathos the stories of senior citizens who have chosen to spend their last years in a place such as Sunny Acres.

Robert Frost once said when he was asked how he started a poem, "I begin with a corner of a thought." What I have done is similar. I have taken slivers of character traits and events and molded them to fit my purpose in telling a story. My point of view is not conventional in that my third person narrator has a dual role. She is a character in the sequence of events and at the same time a writer who is in the process of writing a story about Sunny Acres.

My special thanks go to the residents and staff of Brandon Wilde who have given me enthusiastic support. Two of them, Susie and Jerry Saul, appear on the cover. The photographer is George Clark. Special appreciation goes to my dining room partners: Alva Faulkner, Patricia Mangum, Anne Galloway, Lois Ellison, Jane Peacock, and Martha King. Virginia Tillson proofread the manuscript, and Jane Ball was always around to push me to finish.

THE CURTAIN RISES

All the world's a stage,
And all the men and women merely players;
They have their exits and their entrances...
Shakespeare's As You Like It, *Act II, Scene 7*

Weather prophets of old, without benefit of Doppler or satellites, were wont to scrutinize the evening sky to plan the morrow. Many years hence, after dinner, Ruth Smith, taking her long-haired Chihuahua for his nightly pilgrimage, notes splashes of gold across the west. "Mama would say that the rain is gone. Tomorrow will be sunny," she murmurs. Othello raises his black head to question his mistress. Does she have a treat in her pocket? Not seeing one, he drops his head and sniffs a water hydrant. Lifting his leg to leave his mark, he whiffs a silent "I came." Ruth, who is fluent in canine linguistics, smiles. "I came, too, John. I planted a clump of mountain trillium, your favorite flower, but you were not there. It made the granite stone seem warmer. How long ago was it?" Othello looks at his mistress uncomprehending. "Time like a river flows on," she whispers. "So be it, honey bunch. It's time to go home." A gentle tug on Othello's retractable leash directs him across an expanse of green lawn toward a patio door with countless twins.

This is Sunny Acres, with iron gates and round-the-clock security to protect its residents who live in remnants of their pasts—in every unit there are scraps of younger days and younger voices with Chippendale from great grandma or Havilland wedding china for special occasions. Sunny Acres, despite its name, is not always cloudless. For a few of those residing in its sheltered compounds, bright skies make little difference, but Ruth believes old Sol has magic. She walks sprightly for an octogenarian but pauses briefly to pluck a clump of grass that has invaded her tuberous begonias flourishing in an urn among an array of spring blossoms. The tulips have seen their best days although a few still stand defying time. A sharp twerp issues from a basket of Boston fern. "Who is invading whom?" she inquires as a sparrow flies out in protest. "It's my basket, not yours. Can't you find a tree for your love nest?" She closes the door on No.182 as Othello gives a goodnight yelp to creatures of the darkness that he imagines are lurking outside. Ruth bends to unsnap his leash and stands for a moment to survey her indoor domain. She counts ten plants—philodendron, ivy, fern, cactus, and some she can't name—that have transformed her living room into a miniature jungle. All I need, she thinks, is a monkey to jump from plant to plant. Othello breaks her reverie with the sharp reminder that it's time for a treat and heads toward the cabinet where he knows his favorites are kept. "You are my monkey," she says, as he grabs the proffered goodie from her hand. "No, just one." She smiles at the wagging tail and the hope in two bright eyes. Turning toward her blue recliner, she settles herself comfortably. Her laptop rests on the side table. Disconsolate, Othello moves toward the cushion at her feet. Soon he dozes and does not hear his mistress whisper: "*Sunny Acres. A* story behind every door." She reaches for the laptop and raises the cover. "Where shall I begin?" Her fingers hover over the black keyboard and slowly begin making words. It is a tale told by a retired English teacher, not full of sound and fury like the Bard of Stratford's tales. Hers will be the story of those who are near the end of life, many heroically and fearlessly. She will handle them gently and touch them with humor and sometimes sadness.

Now it is morning, and dreamless sleep has energized Othello. He waits impatiently for the familiar click of the leash on his collar. Together they walk into the cool April air. Not a cloud in the sky. Mama still speaks from her grave; Ruth smiles, because this morning in Sunny Acres is indeed springtime—a southern spring, demanding a walk through nature's garden resplendent in color and joyful in sound.

A winding road bordered by green lawns quilted in patches of pansies edges the woods where tall oaks interspersed with dogwood stand sentinel along a nature trail. Ruth and Othello spot George Clark, an early riser. He formed that habit during his years as a doctor along with usually being in a rush, but today he is in no hurry. He ambles leisurely across the nearby footbridge over a gurgling stream. A hat with a sun visor flattens his mass of white hair. He pauses and studies the weathered oak boards at his feet. Now he lifts his hat. Is he paying mock obeisance to the gray squirrel just ahead who is chattering nonsense, or is he stopping to eavesdrop on the message a red cardinal sends to his mate? The squirrel scurries through a clump of wild daffodils and does not see the tears in George's gray eyes nor hear him softly whisper "Molly." Ruth restrains Othello's interest in the squirrel and admonishes him gently not to interrupt George's reverie. She deliberately guides him toward a favorite tree out of sight of George, who is about to run into Richard Blair.

Richard is an English transplant to Sunny Acres. His daughter, who married an American golfer now retired, lives in nearby Garden City. It was she who brought her father to his adopted country after having persuaded him to close Book Finders. For three generations bibliophiles had browsed its shelves, some of which housed first editions behind locked glass doors. Richard is the last male of the long Blair line. He misses those ancient tomes; at times he even misses the London fog. Now he relishes springtime in the South when the climate more nearly matches home. Leaning upon his cane, he salutes his friend George with his left hand.

"Top of the morning, mate!" Twin nests of bushy gray brows hang over black-rimmed glasses, magnifying mischievous blue eyes. These are eyes that have perused scholarly tomes and perhaps have found mischief even there. His greeting is in good-old-boy English. "A bloke can't miss a morning like this, can he? Your bloody summers are as hot as hell."

"Well, I'll be a son of a gun, Dick. That hip replacement can't get a good man down. I thought you would still be in therapy. Looks like you've put on a few pounds. Have those nurses been fixing you high tea twice a day, giving you that tender loving care? Got to live one day at a time, pal. You and I might be in an even hotter place by summer." He chuckles heartily. "Can't never tell. Guess I'll pay Uncle Sam just to be on the safe side." George places a neighborly pat on a scrawny shoulder. There is no sign of bereavement now, but a certain set in his gray eyes lacks his normal ease.

"Can't complain." Richard's voice takes on a more serious tone. "How about you, George? Sorry I couldn't make it to the service."

"Gonna make it, man. Gonna make it. Soon as you kick that cane, let's have a few holes at the club. You read too damn much. Leave Diogenes in his tub and let Socrates drink his hemlock in peace. Your legs, not your brain, need exercise."

"Right-o. My Tiger swing needs a warm-up."

Ruth watches the two disappear around a curve of pear trees. Their extravagant display of white blooms might trick one into thinking an untimely snow has invaded spring. She wonders if Richard misses England's first spring blooms. One day she just might engineer a conversation: *"O, to be in England now that April's there."* Just see if he knows I'm quoting Browning.

Farther down the trail Biddy Pritchett and Anna Faulk emerge from their constitutional and take their seats on a bench to watch the water ripple from a fountain. Masses of red and white azaleas guard the small nearby lake. Neither of the ladies speaks. The uphill path they have just climbed has left them a bit breathy. Anna is a statuesque figure with a becoming blonde tint to fluffy hair kept in place in a French twist. Alert blue eyes sweep the rose garden nearby as she breaks the silence.

"Look, Biddy. The wind last night has played havoc with the roses." She points toward the garden in which Queen Elizabeth and her celebrated ladies-in-waiting stand upright facing the morning sun despite having some of their petals strew their feet. "Our work is cut out for us Saturday," Anna continues. "I wish you would join the rose group, Biddy. We have lots of fun grooming the garden."

"Have you heard the latest, Anna?" Biddy is interested in neither horticulture nor gardening. This morning her miniature figure sports a bright floral pantsuit, the closest she ever got to a garden. Eyes sharp and alert, they had spotted George and Richard. Now that the two men are not in view, she leans her salon red curls closer to her companion and whispers. "Betty Keaton is now keeping late hours with George Clark. Sylvia Fry saw her leaving his room at midnight. In her robe! Poor Molly Clark is hardly cold in her grave."

Ruth, catching the portent of Biddy's news and not wishing to join in the discussion, waves and continues walking toward the wellness center. Othello makes an unsuccessful dash toward Biddy, for whom he had developed a strange dislike even on their first meeting. Ruth smiles as she rights him in the opposite direction and whispers to his canine ears, "Othello, we leave gossip and porn to fiction. You know that, buddy boy. Think I should interview Biddy for *Sunny Acres*? When I write about her, I could put her in overalls and give her a spade. Nobody would recognize her then." The two wander toward the wellness center and do not hear Anna's bland response to Biddy's gossip.

Anna smiles mildly. "Oh, well, that's their business. Maybe it's because he misses Molly so much. You know Betty and her husband, Ted, were the Clarks'

7

neighbors. Their children played together. He needs companionship right now."

"Humph! Companionship my eye! More like bedship."

Anna shrugs annoyance and announces quickly, "Time for my aerobics, Biddy. Ready to go in?"

"Bend left—turn right. Right foot—turn left. Good!" Pandora, the tall sylph-like figure, smiles broadly. Her black hair pinned back in a ponytail is still wet from an earlier aerobics class. This is Pump-it-Up Class. And Pandora, unlike the mythical figure after whom she is named, is not a troublemaker but a muscle maker who aims to squeeze the last bit of energy from her assemblage of oldsters. Now Anna has joined these early risers. What diversity! Her eyes sweep the motley crew. Sweat suits from Wal-Mart. Designer jeans from The Gap. There are retired doctors, lawyers, teachers and engineers, but no Indian chiefs except for the military who never tire and who would gladly modify the exercise to make it more demanding. There is also diversity in reaction to the exercise as some plod through while others stretch old limbs enthusiastically.

At the other end of the gym, some watch the Pump-it-Ups as they ride stationery bicycles, lift weights, and stretch muscles on machines designed to lessen the possibility of falls, straighten humped backs, and hopefully delay osteoporosis for at least five years.

"Time out!" Pan calls. Water time. Dr. Amanda Goldstein sips from a paper cup and sidles over to

Anna to finalize plans for an early dinner so that they will be ready for the Sunny Acres bus charioting music lovers to the symphony. The doctor, a slight form in a green sweat suit, is Sunny Acres' scholar in science and art and the mother of a family of geniuses. She and her husband, who is now deceased, trekked every corner of the globe in the interest of medicine and culture. Nearby, a gray-haired gentlemen, who has just taken up bridge after a career in shuffling law cases to subordinates, is busy soliciting a fourth for a game. A lady whose slim figure seems out of place among the weighty occupies a bicycle and pedals madly next to Ruth Smith, who is on a stationary machine. Ruth believes time spent here is time doing penance. She hates exercise and the food which is good for her but takes good-naturedly her friend's order to accelerate. Ruth smirks playfully at the petite mentor whose blonde L'Oreal hair is encased in a white turban. Of an age that she refuses to reveal, she faithfully keeps her daily workouts and maintains her schoolgirl figure. Ruth, who has never been a femme fatale with model measurements, returns to perusing *Vanity Fair* and deliberately cuts down the speed on Nutra-Drive as she lackadaisically resumes her pedaling. There is an ongoing friendly duel between the beauty and the ugly duckling, and their repartee enlivens the daily ordeal. At least it is that way for Ruth, who prefers books to bridge, ideas to gossip, and pets to most Homo sapiens. At the same time she is an outspoken friend of the underdog and a staunch defender of the ACLU, beliefs which make her an oddity among the good republicans. A basically kind community, Sunny Acres tolerates Ruth and dismisses her with a casual cliché— *there's one in every crowd.*

Once class is over, a few of the athletes stroll across the lawn to the nurse's office for blood pressure checks. Not Ruth. A victim of *white coat syndrome,* she tries her best to avoid the blood pressure sleeve and submits to its punishment only in her doctor's office. The more obedient class members await their turn while watching others file into a cubby hole large enough for the hospital leech, who is equipped with a tourniquet and syringe, and a single chair for the patient awaiting the dread needle. Sunny Acres provides for its residents' periodic blood tests which are required by doctors.

Caramel, a reddish blonde from the beauty salon, pokes her head in the door to remind Margie Thompson not to be late for her hair color. The nurse wonders silently how much blacker Margie's hair can get. Down the hall in the skilled nursing unit, the clatter of china and the rolling of carts advertise the business of serving breakfast in Rest Haven. Just as the nurse speaks her parting words to Margie—

"That wasn't too bad, was it Mrs. Thompson?"—a thin scream erupts nearby and sends both nurse and patient flying into the hall.

Security guards flank a small woman clad in a floor-length white nightgown with a hand towel draped over lank gray hair. She struggles desperately to free herself. A small gathering watches silently.

"Lemme go! I'm gonna be late. Joe and the preacher are waiting."

"Of course, they are, Mrs. Hendrix," says one of the guards. Another one drops her hand and offers his elbow gallantly. "We'll take you there. Don't worry. This way." They steer her through the door leading outside.

"Thank you." Her misty blue eyes smile at her usher as she makes her way up her make-believe aisle. He bears no resemblance to her father, but like Blanche in *The Streetcar Named Desire,* she, too, believes in the kindness of strangers. She tucks a stray strand of hair behind one ear and adjusts her would-be veil. The door opens gently and the procession progresses outward.

Nobody laughs. Everyone moves quietly back to resume activities. Margie Thompson clutches the Band-Aid on her arm and ambles down to the beauty salon. The nurse whispers to her new patient as she fastens the tourniquet. "Poor Mrs. Hendrix! She's managed to slip out of the Arbor again."

Down the hall in the clubroom George Clark pours Betty Keaton a cup of coffee freshly brewed for the residents. Betty, in her late seventies, could pass for fifty. Light brown hair artfully devoid of tell-tale gray frames an unwrinkled face. Her gray eyes are warm and match the smile she wears as she greets everyone by name. That smile now lights up for George as he guides her to a vacant table. Half a dozen pairs of eyes, including Ruth's, follow them. The writer is not above eavesdropping. She notes the mild amusement suffusing George's face and smiles knowingly as his otherwise sober face relaxes. He reaches over to pat Betty's hand. She smiles wickedly and whispers, "Who would have thought that borrowing a hot water bottle could cause such a stir? Sunny Acres is having such fun. I replaced my old one yesterday. Don't spoil it for them, George. Somebody should write a book about this place."

"I'll never tell. I just love it," he whispers back.

It is hard for Ruth to control her laughter. "Another tidbit for a novel in progress," Ruth murmurs. She eyes Biddy Pritchett, who has stopped by on the way to the mailbox. Undoubtedly Biddy will declare later to eager listening ears that she had heard George Clark make a declaration of love to Betty and will end with "What's the world coming to?"

What has the world come to for four hundred odd persons in Sunny Acres? It is a modern complex of apartments and cottages situated on one hundred and three acres in a moderately sized Georgia town spreading out along the shores of the Savannah River. Under the watchful eyes of a professionally trained staff, the residents represent a divergence of culture and circumstance. Ages range from sixty-two to one hundred five. There are pockets which are pension slender, and there are portfolios stuffed with blue chips. Mobility varies from bed rest, to four-wheeled walkers, scooters to spirited jogging, and daily attendance to the wellness center to lying in bed until mid-morning. There are smiles and a few scowls, for most have accepted Sunny Acres as their new home, a kind of club where bridge, meals, cocktails and shopping (via the bus) are available. The more venturesome may elect spins in their cars or find respite from daily routine on cruises and trips abroad. Others are content to travel vicariously through books or the Internet.

Ruth Smith is one of the latter. A retired English teacher, she is one of the many bibliophiles of Sunny Acres. She is not even mildly curious as to whether George is cohabiting with Betty. Human nature is amusing, not shocking. What one is thinking or reading is more interesting. However, she watches the scenes around her, a serial with such a large cast of characters that she cannot identify them all; therefore, those she knows less well she pigeonholes into stereotypes to which she thinks they belong. Among these she names the social climber, the man hunter, and the exclusive cliques. And, of course, there is the gossip, dear old Biddy, whose first misfortune was to be nicknamed Biddy, because at birth she weighed only four pounds. It is not to say that Ruth lacks perception and compassion; she can easily spot the sadness that lurks behind a smile or the empty laughter that hides a hurt. She often thinks that if she were a painter, she would like to capture Sunny Acres on frescoed walls, but even the Sistine Chapel would not be capacious enough to accommodate the population loitering on the Stygian shores. Death bells, however, are muted here and an exodus is treated with formality and dignity.

Such are Ruth's meanderings as she wends toward the lobby and a comfortable seat on a sofa. Anna Faulk strolls in. "Hello, Ruth. Not reading?"

"No, just wool gathering."

"You sound like a sheep herder, Ruth."

"You Yankees! Wool gathering is an old southern idiom. I mean I'm just daydreaming—thoughts disconnected. Anyway, how is that toe? And how was your jaunt with Biddy? Is there anything newsworthy?" Ruth smiles, knowing full well the headlines in Biddy's journal.

"It's almost well. The toe, that is." Anna smiles, "At our age, Ruth, every day brings another ache in a new location. Speaking of Biddy, I grant you she has imagination. I think all her talk comes from boredom. You must admit she keeps Sunny Acres lively."

"You are certainly right about that. Her news mill feeds my new book. Don't misunderstand. I'm not out to hurt Biddy or anyone else at Sunny Acres. I'll just take a sliver of Biddy and cast her in a pearl, imperfect but still a gem. That's what makes writing fun, and the research is easy. I just watch people come and go."

The couch upon which Ruth and Anna sit faces a fireplace; on cool mornings or evenings cheerful sparks cascade from man-made logs ignited by gas. From this vantage point the automatic sliding glass doors of the foyer are visible. Through them a steady stream of staff and residents go in and out. With one eye Ruth surveys the traffic, and she listens as Anna describes the state of her once-infected digit. Biddy Pritchett steps off the lobby elevator and interrupts an inspired discussion of Anna's favorite over-the-counter miracle healing creme.

"Betsy Hendrix got out again. She was a picture for sore eyes parading in her nightgown, thinking she was heading to her wedding. Those attendants in her wing sure don't earn their pay."

"Oh, come off it, Biddy," Anna interposes mildly. "They are probably understaffed this morning. A bug has been going around. Anyway, Betsy does no harm. She wouldn't hurt a flea." Anna exchanges looks with Ruth, who shrugs impatiently.

"It may be Betsy has been reading *Great Expectations* and imagines she is Miss Haversham in her wedding dress," Ruth suggests.

"I don't know anything about Abersam or whatever you call her, but the only expectation that woman has is the loony bin."

"May be that's where I belong," Ruth smiles. "Yesterday, I couldn't remember where I had put my hearing aid. Found it safely stored in its box in the refrigerator. I'll see if I can get a cell next to Betsy. Want to join us, Anna? We could be called the three looneyteers."

Anna chuckles. Biddy scowls and turns abruptly

to waylay her next door neighbor, Sylvia Fry, who is heading toward the mailbox to post a handful of letters. As the two are fond of trading gossip, Biddy is quite sure she will have an ally in her point of view about Betsy. Instead, Sylvia pauses to commiserate with Ruth. The two of them have frequently shared stories of their dogs' antics.

"You know," Sylvia confides, "I lost my hearing aid. Guess what. I found it in three pieces. Caesar thought it was one of his chicken treats. I'm sure glad I had insurance on it."

"I'm sure you are," Ruth said.

"What did you say, Ruth? I can't hear a thing in all this noise. My new hearing aid hasn't come yet." Not waiting to get a response, she ambles off with Biddy trailing behind to fill her in on the Betsy story.

Ruth turns to Anna. "I'm sure Sylvia's ears are good enough to hear Biddy's pitch, with or without a hearing aid."

"I think Biddy is just bored, Ruth. I don't think she means to hurt people."

"You are always so charitable Anna. I think Biddy is Mrs. Turpin straight out of 'Revelation,' a Flannery O'Connor short story. Suppose I send her a copy. Think she would recognize herself?"

"Biddy doesn't have enough to do. I feel rather sorry for her."

"Then why don't you to teach her to play bridge and get her into your group?"

"Ruth!"

"I'm just kidding, Anna. Oh, here comes a walking saint. He is such a sweet man. He's so attentive to his wife. I hear he gets her out of Rest Haven each morning and takes her to his apartment in independent living. I wonder if Biddy could find some kind words for him."

"Well, she knows all about how their son neglects them. I can't help agreeing with Biddy when she lays into him."

"I know. I taught the young man. Brilliant! He was translating Virgil on his own when he was in elementary school and then became the youngest freshman ever to enter Yale. Now he has a doctorate in theology and is the head of a department at a seminary. His dad says they have not heard from him in ten years. I wonder what his lectures on apologetics are like."

"There's no understanding such heartlessness. Changing the subject, I want to ask if you are planning to go to the symphony tonight? You may have my ticket. It's my great-grandson's birthday and we're celebrating at the club. He's our first boy in a family of mostly girls."

"Thanks, Anna, but no. I decided to stay home to do a bit of writing. That is, if the muse cooperates. Besides, the program tonight is so modern. I just don't like dissonance. My tastes in music got stuck in the Nineteenth Century. My musical education has a deficit."

"You mean you don't like Copeland or Bernstein?" The speaker is Dr. Goldstein, whose sharp ears compensate for the macular degeneration in her eyes. Her nose, equally as sensitive as her ears, can differentiate between California Kroger wine and the aged spirits of France or Italy. Now she smiles at Ruth's preference in music. "I suppose my tastes are more eclectic. My husband and I even enjoyed Chinese opera in Beijing. Ruth, you . . ."

Her words are cut short by a flicker of lights, and then the lobby is plunged into semi-darkness. For those assembled in the Sunny Acres general room taking the driving course to update discounts in car insurance, the darkness is palpable. Carmen Brodsky feels for her four-carat diamond temporarily discarded in order to exercise her arthritic finger. The ring has a history that everyone has heard. Once it belonged to a gangster who was killed by Al Capone, who wrested it from the dying man's finger. Eventually it graced the hand of Capone's lady, who pawned it for a ticket out west to escape the Mafia. A railroad man, who had struck it rich, retrieved it from the ignorant ticket agent. He put it on his bride's finger. After three more generations of fingers, the ring became the possession of Carmen Brodsky, whose eyes fill with tears every time she looks at it, not in memory of Al Capone, but of her beloved husband who died prematurely at the age of ninety-two. He left a bride of less than forty and a ring now valued at fifty thousand. The stone, sturdy as the carbon from which it was chiseled, has outlasted two additional husbands whom Carmen remembers fondly but not quite so tenderly as her first spouse.

After several minutes in darkness, Sunny Acres is re-illuminated and shown in moderate chaos with people trapped in elevators and doors refusing to open. Biddy Pritchett, who has made it to her room, searches for her diamond bracelet, feeling sure that Al Qaeda has landed and that she along with the rest of Sunny Acres is about to be robbed of wallets, family heirlooms, and any other valuables that terrorists can lay their Muslim hands on. She breathes a momentary sigh of relief as she clutches the bracelet and secures it in the cup of her bra.

Just as maintenance is about to fire up the generator, somebody out there says, "Let there be light and there was light and it was good." The restorer, however, is not the Creator but three hefty policemen who manage to extricate an ancient oak from a light pole. Life in Sunny Acres resumes: Biddy transfers her bracelet from her bra to a new hidey hole, Amanda resumes her pontification on the new trends in music, and Carmen Brodsky discovers that her four-carat diamond, valued at fifty thousand but worth twice that much she thinks, is no longer lying by the computer on which she has been lately viewing what happens to a car which endeavors to pass in the right lane.

A scream emanates from the red-lipped Carmen. Somebody mistakes the sound for a fire alarm and yells, "Well, what in the world is going to happen next?"

What happens next is bedlam in the general

conference room. The black patrolman, who has been teaching the driving course, believes his student Carmen has just suffered a coronary. He rushes to her side and is met with, "You black son of a bitch! Where is my diamond?"

THE DIAMOND FOUND

A horror descends upon the once quiet, peaceful community. Lieutenant Armstrong, his mouth agape, his white teeth shining in the black cavern of his face, stands transfixed as though waiting for an ancient noose. Twenty ladies and four gentlemen eye the victim and the accused. A stunned silence immobilizes their tongues. The chaplain-in-residence strides from his office next door toward the congregation of shocked residents, ill-prepared either to deliver a sermon on racial tolerance or to quiet an eighty-year-old female now screaming, "Police! Police!"

Lieutenant Armstrong stoops at Carmen's knee. Is he mockingly kneeling to Her Majesty? No, he is reaching down and calmly fishing out a gleaming stone lodged between the straps of her black sandal. He holds the gleaming eye in the palm of his hand and smiles.

"I am the police, madam," he says calmly as he proffers the diamond.

The impact of the words she had earlier yelled at him explodes in her brain. She clasps her breasts and gasps out a dying request for forgiveness. She is sure that her pacemaker is on the blink and at the moment wishes with all her soul that it has stopped. One hand clutches her ample bosom which moves spasmodically as she gasps.

The army is coming. A former General steps up smartly, pulls the languishing lady from her chair and steers her to the door. At the door the General makes a military salute to the Lieutenant, who returns it expertly. Too bad that Biddy Pritchett is not there, but news travels as fast as email at Sunny Acres.

Another noble rescue to the General's credit! Sunny Acres thrills to his story about a little Korean lad, caught between armies and separated from his parents during a raging battle. The good General, Commander of the 24th Regiment, scoops up the weeping child. Ten months later he was able to transfer the little boy into the arms of his parents. Now the young man is a prosperous developer in Florida. Once caught between the forces of war, he remembers his benefactor with affection. Sunny Acres is cordial to the successful businessman who brings his family to visit the beloved general.

Ruth Smith watches as the General guides the weeping Mrs. Brodsky down the hall to the nurse's office. "Did you hear what Carmen called that black policeman?" somebody whispers. Ruth leans toward the speaker to hear what would make coffee breaks and even the bridge table for weeks tingle in electric repartee.

Sunny Acres is a gold mine in stories. If only she could do the residents justice on paper. What marvelous tales could be woven into a tapestry depicting the human situation? Not exactly like the sacred frescoes in the Sistine Chapel, but no less interesting. Too bad she was not present to witness the scenario. Nevertheless, stories spread like wildfire in dry timber with details to embellish the scene. Ruth opens her daily log kept in a little black notebook and strokes a few notes. Timber, indeed, for her house of tales in progress.

Just the other day a long-time resident of Sunny Acres showed her a picture of a 1989 Chevrolet Impala. "This is the *get-away* car. One of our ninety year olds got tired of the hospital. He phoned his best friend, who was just eighty-eight, to rescue him. Would you believe that the old fellow crept down the fire escape in his hospital gown which, incidentally, was not tied in the back, and slipped undetected into the waiting car?"

"I don't believe you," Ruth laughed. "That is stuff and nonsense."

"Stuff and nonsense, my eye. I could tell you tales that not only would tickle your funny bone but also would make your hair curl."

"Then tell me."

"You wouldn't believe me anyway, Ruth. There is a story in every corner of Sunny Acres. They're better than all those books you've read, or all those other novels you keep saying you're going to write."

Yes, books had been companions all of Ruth's life. She had even managed two publications printed by a small independent press. These two coming-of-age novels spawned from a childhood in the Low Country of South Carolina clearly marked Ruth Smith as a feminist, a liberal by conservative standards, actually one who could look at both sides of the coin and one who did not make her decisions with a casual flip. There was no doubt that she was a spokeswoman for human rights. Never in her wildest imagination could she envision a response like Carmen Brodsky's. Unless, of course, she witnessed the abuse of an animal, an act that would turn the pacifist Ruth into a violent woman. She had often pontificated to her students on the superiority of dogs. Not God's lesser creatures by any means. Who among us can find other humans who have never revealed a confidence, have never held a grudge, and have loved unconditionally? There had been laughter from her classes, but they knew that their teacher's words were not uttered in jest.

These are Ruth's random thoughts as she strolls into the dining room for an early lunch. Eating early will provide her uninterrupted time to fight with the muse, but today there should be no struggle to find something to say. Poor Carmen! She must find a way to make the incident less painful should *Sunny Acres* be read. Perhaps she should leave it out entirely. It surely would make a good story, but Carmen has suffered enough. There are the self-righteous ones like Biddy, who will not let Carmen forget. Of course, they will say nothing to her. Instead, there will be little conspiratorial glances and whispers that will not escape poor Carmen. Yes. Kindest to leave it out.

Alicia, the trim hostess who always looks so professional in her tailored jacket coordinated with her trousers, stands smiling in the doorway to the dining room. Ruth ambles in along with others for an early lunch. Some do not amble but arrive on scooters, walkers, and crutches or come assisted by canes. Many join a daily companion while a few sit alone, perhaps hoping that a stray diner might join them. Ruth welcomes the possibility of an interesting chat, but solitude does not bother her particularly. She simply creates an interior dialogue that might involve conflicting reactions to something she has heard, read or contemplated writing.

The dining room is elegant with its linen tablecloths, artistic flower arrangements and waiters and waitresses in shirts and ties. For many generations, grandmoms and granddads moved into cramped quarters with sometimes reluctant children, but now they have another option. Sunny Acres provides a new concept. Science having added to longevity, many oldsters have choices—not a nursing abode to await the grim reaper, but the possibility of a home with many of the accoutrements of the ones they will leave. How had all of this begun? Certainly there had been a master plan. Sunny Acres is listed as one of the top twenty of such residences for the older generation who live and enjoy life much longer. Independent living gives way to assisted living, and for some, the next step is skilled nursing care in Rest Haven. Poor Betsy Hendrix, who periodically imagines being late for her wedding, and Ida, Ruth's friend who yearns for her home, live in the Arbor, a beautiful wing to Sunny Acres. It has an unobstructed view of tall maples through which the sun freckles the grass in shadows. The Arbor offers two worlds—a peaceful exterior and the anxious interior of minds like Betsy's and Ida's. For the elderly, Sunny Acres is a sensible and pleasant lifestyle which leaves relatives free to lead their own lives. Now Ruth surveys the dining room for a table.

"I do not believe this soup has been near a stove in twenty-four hours. You must have a crammed refrigerator to accommodate it all. Don't you have a microwave in the kitchen?" The speaker is Biddy Pritchett. Picking up her soup bowl, she thrusts it toward Akela, sloshing the soup on the once-spotless tablecloth.

Akela rescues the bowl before it can do more damage. A smile spreads across her pleasant brown face as she surveys Biddy's table companions. Anna Faulk is making every effort to suppress a smile while

Betty Keaton pays studious attention to her salad. "I'm so sorry, Mrs. Pritchett. I thought you ordered Vichyssoise. You know it's supposed to be served cold. If you prefer the clam chowder, I am sure it will be served nice and hot."

Biddy blushes even under her rouge. She who claims to be a direct descendent from Elizabeth I has made a terrible faux pas. Desperate to recover the esteem of her friends, she replies, "I did order the clam chowder. And yes, I would like it hot."

Ruth smiles unobserved and thinks upon Biddy. Such a sad person! She must be very lonely and insecure—always trying to impress by extolling the virtues of her late husband who had made a mint in real estate and enumerating her noble ancestors that stretch back into royalty. Nobody has enlightened her about Good Queen Bess's unmarried state. Well, just wait until she delivers her genealogy to Dr. Goldstein. That could be a scene to evoke laughter. Well, maybe not. Not even Biddy in her last years deserves ridicule from Ruth Smith's pen. But yes, a story behind every door.

"Good morning, Ruth. May I join you?" Bill says as he approaches. "Nancy's sitting with the grands this week so I'm on my own. She left me instructions to behave myself but to be kind to all these lonely widows."

"Well, if you are ready to give solace to a grieving widow, you had better seek another table."

"Come now. Nancy didn't have a thing to say about unmarried English teachers. Besides, you taught our children. So, I am not required to behave or to be kind. In fact, I can switch roles and be the teacher. Why don't you go to exercise regularly? It's good for you."

"It's like taking castor oil that my mother used to give me in orange juice. I have said many times that death would be sweet in comparison. Don't fuss at me, Bill. I go enough to keep me on my feet and off a scooter. I'm old enough now to indulge my whims."

"You haven't changed a bit, Miss Smith. Still the character that my children hated when they had you and later loved once they got to college. Do you miss the classroom, Ruth?"

"Do you miss being a CEO?"

"Yes, as a matter of fact I do. But, you know, Ruth, as I walk around Sunny Acres, I often relive those good old days. I remember when Sunny Acres was truly thirty-five acres of oaks, pine, and sweet gum with a ranch-style house perched on a knoll near a pond. Golly, how time flies! Who would have thought that a single phone call to my office at St. Joseph Hospital would have culminated in all of this?" He spreads his arms in a sweeping gesture to embrace not only the Sunny Acres dining room but its environs.

Ruth lifts her spoon to taste the Vichyssoise that had just been served and looks at the man in front of her. Bill Armstrong has weathered the years well with the physique and stride of a much younger man and no evidence of the usual paunch. Although his hair is not so abundant as when she had first met him at parent-teacher's night many, many years ago, his blue eyes have retained their sparkle, and there is no pronounced need of a face lift to tighten sagging skin. She remembers when she first encountered him in Sunny Acres. He was trying to solicit three males to form a quartet. She had suggested her little dog, Othello, who demonstrates a healthy tenor voice when he accompanies her in the Hallelujah Chorus. Although Bill declined the offer even after hearing Othello perform, there had been no hard feelings. Besides, he likes dogs and on one occasion had written a charming expose of the dogs and their masters and mistresses at Sunny Acres.

"You know, Bill, I've just been thinking about how it all got started. In fact, I'm actually doing some writing about a place like this one. Someone said to me just this morning that there is a story behind every door. I bet there's quite a story about the people on the ground floor who planned it. And what a unique concept! Was it original with the planners of Sunny Acres?"

"Well, Ruth, it's a long story; it's an exciting story. Let me order one of those fattening Sunny Acres hamburgers while Nancy is not here to watch my diet. She can count calories faster than a bank teller can count money."

"You should be grateful. That's the reason for your schoolboy figure. But come on. How did it all get started?"

A smile spreads across his face. He taps his head lightly as though trying to recall something important. "Let me see. I think it was around 1985. It was just another day at St. Joseph—the regular headaches for a CEO along with watching the good things around me. The Sisters of Carondelet—then you could tell they were sisters; no mistaking them in their starched attire—were stopping by my office to chat or to express concerns. It was just an ordinary day. Then the telephone rang."

Bill continues, "I lifted the phone and groaned thinking it was the announcement of another meeting. A voice I couldn't identify said, 'Mr. Armstrong, this is Jim Culpepper. You know how Augusta is spreading out into Columbia County. I thought maybe St. Joseph might be interested in a piece of property out there. I'd really like to see those sisters carry on their work out this way. It's about thirty-five acres. My wife and I have decided to sell it. We're both getting up in years. We thought maybe you might like to come out and take a look at it.' I asked him where it was located. I took a look at my watch. I told him I would meet him in an hour. Why did I jump so quickly? Well, the reason is that the story goes back to around 1982—or maybe '83."

"Before you go back three years, you had better take a bite of that burger that's coming."

"Forever the school marm, Miss Smith. You interrupt me to give orders just as you've been doing all your life."

"Not all my life, I hope. Okay. I'll listen while you talk even if your mouth is full. What happened back in '83?"

"Well, seven of us interested commissioners and CEOs met to talk about the need for an additional hospital—one to serve the rapid growth in Columbia County. Some of us saw the new hospital just as an investment; others were just as interested in the service as well as the surplus money coming in. St. Joseph, for example, thought in terms of extending the work of Christ. Sister Rose Margaret, in particular, considered it a spiritual mission."

"But, Bill, this is a far cry from what actually evolved. We now have independent living, assisted living and even skilled nursing care. How did all this come about from the idea of an additional hospital?"

"As I said, it's a long story. And it's still continuing. Plans are being made for a new Arbor. The idea is to make a more homey atmosphere for residents with Alzheimer's disease and dementia. Let's continue this another day. I have a meeting and the story of Sunny Acres is a long one."

Ruth looks at her watch. "And I promised to read to somebody who is now in nursing care. She used to be as addicted to books as I am. Poor thing! She now has macular degeneration and is dependent on listening tapes. I go by and visit with her, read the obituaries in the paper and sometimes take along a short story to share and then discuss with her. I need to earn a few brownie points. Besides, I enjoy the visits. But, seriously, let's get together so that you continue with this fascinating history. I will bring along a notebook. I'm being very serious. I am planning to weave *Sunny Acres* into the lives of some remarkable people who live here."

"Okay. But if you make a mint of money, I want my cut."

On the way to Assisted Living, Ruth bumps into a former colleague who has just returned from a trip to Scotland, an annual pilgrimage to the land of her birth. Her parents moved to the South when she was just an infant. As one who is very proud of her heritage, she can do an authentic Scottish burr entertaining a coterie of Burns fans. She is also a reader but prefers Scottish writers and settings. She and Ruth share admiration for P. D. James, a writer not Scottish by birth but one who weaves marvelous mysteries in the Highlands. Susie has just returned from a walking tour of the Trossachs that Sir Walter Scott made famous in *The Lady of the Lake*. Ruth would love to hear a description of Loch Lomond or Loch Katrine. Instead, Susie launches into a diatribe about Janie, her Himalayan, who bit her sitter while Susie was on the trip. "It was all Phyllis's fault. I told her that Janie always has a snack at midnight. Phyllis probably interrupted Janie's art work. You know she takes her leftover kittles and uses her paw to make the most marvelous artistic creations. The day I got back, the Eiffel Tower was on her saucer. I guess she thought I had gone to Paris."

Ruth manages to smother a laugh. "Oh, well, all's well that ends well. I know Janie was glad to see you, and Phyllis has probably forgotten all about Janie by now. Our pets miss us when we're away. It may be that Janie thought she was biting you instead of Phyllis. Maybe she was punishing you for leaving her. Let's get together so you can give me a tour of Boswell's stomping grounds."

A smile wreaths Susie's face. She forgets for the moment about Janie's misbehavior and her artistry. She is ready to talk about Scotland. "Yeah, you know what that bastard Johnson said to Boswell. 'The only thing good about Scotland is that it has a road leading to England.'" The two laugh as they remember the famous biographer who immortalized the great Dr. Johnson of the acid tongue. Ruth confides that Sunny Acres has a few wicked Dr. Johnsons although there is no evidence that they are smart enough to write a dictionary. "See you later, Susie. Check your calendar and let's eat together." There are mutual nods of approval as Ruth heads down the hall. Well, she thinks, Janie's building the Eiffel Tower is no more far-fetched than Othello's singing the Hallelujah Chorus.

TRADING WALKING
STICKS FOR CROWNS

Ruth and Othello sit on their small patio and assess life in Sunny Acres. Her attention is divided between the black keys on her computer and a mental survey of the rolling green lawn sliced with curved walkways wide enough to accommodate not only scooters but also golf cars. The landscape artist has done his job well in this semi-forest of trees interspersed with circular beds of begonias and coleus. Man and nature have collaborated. Peace is here, peace and beauty. Othello fixes sharp black eyes on two squirrels skittering along the limbs of a stately white birch. He knows a chase is possible only if their play brings them earthward. Unmindful of their watcher, they scoot too far out on a leafy branch which bends under their weight. Joyfully

Othello leaps onto the lawn and scampers toward his prey, which elude him by clutching onto a lower limb, giving them safety from their would-be pursuer.

Ruth lifts her fingers from the keyboard and contemplates the scene before her. She thinks of her father who saw lessons in everything. Often his words were drops of wisdom strung in a strand of pearls. If only she could transfer her thoughts (sometimes lilting with laughter—sometimes too deep for tears) to the black tabs on her lap which would in turn illuminate them on paper. She has just witnessed a bit of play from nature's furry creatures and a bit of disappointment of one denied a chase. How quickly Othello has recovered! His wagging tail forgives them—a lesson that man's best friend might teach his master. How wonderful is this little canine. His greatest gift is the capacity to love unconditionally and to live in the eternal now. Would that the residents of Sunny Acres could be so lucky!

Through the trees Ruth spots Nan and Joseph Lawrence, a couple who celebrated their sixty-seventh wedding anniversary just last week. All Sunny Acres turned out to help them and their children celebrate at the clubhouse. Joseph was the star entertainer as he reminisced about their colorful past. They had met in their teens, and for them it was love at first sight. Then it was 1941. Then came Pearl Harbor and the stirring words of FDR—"*a date which will live in infamy.*" Joseph was one of the first to volunteer. Then it was spring again and birthday time, and Joseph was on leave before going overseas. Their wedding, much disapproved by parents, was performed by a justice of the peace in a courthouse still bearing scars from the war that divided America and turned cousins into enemies. It was a tearful farewell. Nan, who loved Emily Dickinson's poetry, whispered in her young husband's ear—*"Parting is all we know of heaven, And all we need of hell"*—the heaven of being reunited, the hell of separation. Now they walk down the path holding hands, she clasping her cane, he peering through thick lenses but confident she will guide him even as she feels security in the strength of his hand. The goddess of discord, Isis, had not attended their simple exchange of vows; instead, the gods had smiled upon them and had blessed their union. The death of their only son in Vietnam had marred their happiness, but not even death had altered their love. As they make their leisurely approach to Ruth's patio, she remembers that today is their anniversary and also their birthdays.

"Happy Birthday! And Happy Anniversary! I can't believe you two have the same birthday. Still more unbelievable is that you were married on your birthdays. When did you two lovebirds tamper with the calendar? I'm trying to write fiction but even that should be believable."

Joseph chuckles. "Funny thing. Nan's family had just moved into my hometown, a little bump in the road in south Texas. I was sitting in church one Sunday morning watching the girls go by, and I needed a date for the prom the worst way. Two had already turned me down. One said she had already bought three-inch heels and she didn't intend looking down on her date. The other one, a cute little Mexican lass, said her daddy wouldn't let her dance with anyone but her brother. Well, boy, am I glad they had other plans. In comes this girl swishing her hips in a white Easter dress and wearing a big bow on her blonde curls. 'Ma,' I whispered, 'I just found a date for the prom.' She looked at me suspiciously and felt my forehead to see if I had a fever. But I had found courage; after all, I was a man. My new-found confidence marched me right up to this girl after church with an invitation for a club soda at the corner drugstore when it opened at four."

Joseph smiles and keeps going. "'Well,' the girl said—and she had the prettiest smile I'd ever seen— 'my birthday was yesterday, but moving into our new house didn't give us time to celebrate.' 'Guess what! My birthday was yesterday,' I told her. She answered, 'I don't believe it. You're making this up.' Her eyes were as wide as the blue saucers belonging to grandma's china. I convinced her that I'd meet her at the drugstore at four and bring her my birth certificate. And so on a Sunday afternoon in a corner drugstore drinking the second ice cream soda with two straws, I proposed."

"You liar," Nan said. She gives him a gentle slap on his cheek. "It took you ten telephone calls, three movies, and a bottle of Evening in Paris perfume before you got up the nerve."

"Not the way I remembered it."

Ruth laughs. "So you really got married on your birthday?"

"Yep. The war was on. I dropped out of school and volunteered. Nan was still in Teacher's Normal. I knew it was my last leave before overseas. Our folks didn't approve of war marriages. So Nan and I slipped down to the JP and saved them the price of rice-throwing. They forgave us. Fact of the matter they both bought war bonds for our children's education."

"Spring is the season of love and you two belong in it. I still can't believe the romance has been going on for sixty-seven years. What is the appropriate gift, Joseph, to give your wife on that occasion?"

Joseph's blue eyes twinkle. "I don't rightly know, Ruth, but Nan renewed my Viagra prescription and I renewed hers on the Pill."

Nan's fist targets his side. "After all these years, I still have not been able to control his mouth. My gift to him was masking tape, but you can see he still has loose lips."

"I have better use for my lips than covering them with masking tape." He bends and aims a kiss that misses and lands on her cheek. "That wouldn't have happened sixty-seven years ago. We practiced kissing so much that we soon got it just right. Ruth, why don't you put us in that book you are writing?"

"Truth is stranger than fiction. If I put your story into my novel, some editor will say it is contrived." Joseph puts his arm around Nan's waist and smiles.

"It hasn't ended yet," Joseph says solemnly. There is no levity now. Ruth can't be sure, but she thinks she glimpses a tear. "Why don't you write it and give our story a real fairy tale ending?"

"Like what? You two are already a fairy tale."

Nan looks into her husband's eyes and says softly, "That would be nice, wouldn't it?"

Ruth feels a lump in her throat. She is afraid to speak as she watches them, he drawing her close and she smiling into his eyes.

"Ever heard the story of Baucis and Philemon?" Joseph asks. "Read it years ago. It was one of those tales based on Greek myths. I think it was in my fifth grade reader. Funny how you remember what happened in your childhood, and now I can't remember what happened yesterday."

"I know what you mean, Joseph. But yes, I loved all those old myths."

"That's kind of like what Nan and I would like. As I recall this poor couple entertained a stranger, not knowing he was a god. At the end of his visit, the visitor gave them their wish. Remember. They died on the same day."

"If I remember correctly, they didn't die. They just turned into trees standing side by side. Got a favorite tree?"

It is Nan who speaks now. "Oh, I think birches would be nice. I remember Frost's poem. Might be our great grandchildren could find them one day and swing on them."

Ruth whispers the last line of the poem. "One could do worse than be a swinger of birches."

No one speaks. Their arms around each other, Joseph and Nan turn down the path that winds through the trees. Ruth places her fingers on the computer keys, but her eyes follow the couple until they disappear. Minutes pass. Then her fingers begin to move slowly as though they have lost their memory of the keyboard. She is a bit surprised when the word *love* appears on the screen before her.

She finally presses the Enter key and watches the cursor move to a paragraph indention. What can she add to the story of Joseph and Nan? It seems to her that the one word sums it up. She closes her eyes and envisions Frost's slender white birches, *bending to left and right.* She says to no one in particular, "But how fitting—a story with a beautiful beginning and mythical ending. It is the kind that some literary critics will label *trite—unbelievable—sweet romance.* How can a writer capture the tenderness, the loyalty, the simplicity of the good life wrapped in the security of the deepest affection without sounding maudlin?" Now she addresses Othello: "Buddy boy, your missus does not have the talent to weave such a tale." His little black head moves from side to side, desperately trying to interpret the meaning of her words and to understand the pensive face bending above him. Her hand strokes his soft fur to reassure him. He wags his tail and yips a thank you. All is well in this black Othello's world. Unlike Shakespeare's hero, the Moor of Venice, he has no Desdemona and no Iago to make his life miserable.

WOOL GATHERING, COYOTES, AND SPEED TICKETS

In Ruth's apartment is one of those modern clocks that looks like a genuine grandfather, but it is in reality an artifice of some industrial designer in China or Japan who has given it a yellowed face with Roman numerals and a brass pendulum. It ticks soundlessly but tolls the hours and dies mechanically along with two AAA batteries which live in the heart of its mahogany edifice. It has fooled even the antiquarians at Sunny Acres. What they have not observed is the silence of its tongue. Nor do they know that the last chime comes at nine in the evening and the first is at six in the morning. It is a modern adaptation to accommodate those who should be sleeping instead of counting the tick-tocks at midnight. So different from the clock of her childhood whose tick-tocks were unceasing unless someone had forgotten to wind it.

As she hears the syncopated drops of an April shower outside, Ruth's thoughts turn to her childhood home. She recalls the clatter of rain on the tin roof and the back porch with a massive wooden box containing sawdust and a hundred pound block of ice delivered each Friday. "Home," she whispers. "It is the taste of butter just churned. It is cold winter nights with an oak fire in the chimney announcing bedtime with the collapse of logs with embers still glowing over a sheet of ash." And the images in her mind continue. It is the wedding of her niece who has just graduated from college. Ruth, determined to have a proper service in the brand new country church, borrows an organ from the funeral home. That devil of an organist that Ruth imports from Garden City plays as one of his preludes "Come Sweet Death," but nobody identifies it. They are good country people whose Bach is Roy Acuff and the *Grand Old Opry* on the radio Saturday nights. Now the niece is a grandmother; now Ruth is old, and though she cannot remember names, she can see that little blonde bride escaping a rice shower as she flies down the steps with her new husband. And now Sunny Acres. Is this really home? What about the others in Sunny Acres? Is life here a fake—a waiting for the last tick of the clock—the inevitable hour that no one knows, and no one wants to know?

There it is. The prelude to the Westminster Chimes. It is six o'clock and Othello, who is not attuned to the clock, snuggles a bit closer and yips at a friend in dreamland. Ruth waits for a glimmer of gold to shine through the dogwood trees. In the meantime, her thoughts find Ida, her college friend who lives now at Sunny Acres in the Arbor along with Betsy Hendrix. Ida believes that she left home yesterday and is eager to get back. Home is a little two-bedroom house sitting in a drop below the street level, an unpretentious brown wooden structure with a sloping roof. Inside, the physical layout reflects the character of the owner. The Danish modern utilitarian furniture does not fit comfortably with Victorian paintings of Ida's mother, whom she lost when she was only eleven. But the stacks of classical recordings bespeak Ida's inheritance of her mother's love of music. In Sunny Acres Ida now sits by the window; her mind appears blank. She cannot count the years that have passed since she sat in a chair with her mother's painting of *Ruth and Naomi* smiling down on her as she listened to Beethoven and Chopin. She asks, "*Why can't I go home? I want to go home. My bird feeders need filling. I forgot to bring my Christmas cactus in and it's cold tonight.*" She does not see the beauty of her surroundings. Every waking moment she awaits liberation, and her sole greeting to her friend Ruth is "You have come to take me home."

Ruth turns restlessly in her bed and forces her thoughts into pleasanter channels. What she needs is to dress hurriedly and go to the club room for coffee. Many residents like Ruth depend on instant coffee in early morning. It beats washing a pot. But this morning she has a taste for real brew. It's worth getting dressed for a cup of Starbucks. Besides, the club room has other attractions. People. Fodder for *Sunny Acres*. Respite from too many memories.

Although Sunny Acres is the last home for over four hundred senior citizens, for many of them, nostalgia is tempered by curiosity fueled with imagination. Ruth smiles as she pours a fragrant cup of club room special. The rumor mill is running. Perhaps she should have come earlier. She has probably missed the latest gossip. Not to worry, she thinks. Tongues will continue to wag. Just as she sips a cup of steaming brew, Jackson White, an early walker, rushes into the club room.

"I just saw a coyote," says the glad bearer of sensational news.

"Great Caesar's ghost, Jackson, you are in Georgia, not in Texas. What you think you saw was probably a coon or a skunk." This comes from Harry, a hunter, who has stomped the swamps of the Pee Dee to the mountains of Tennessee. He speaks with authority.

Jackson responds the same way: "Look, I may be from Texas, but I ain't George Bush and I can tell a coyote from a skunk."

Betty Keaton, acting as the arbitrator, offers gently in a modulated voice, "Who says Georgia doesn't harbor coyotes? Just last week my sister who lives in Atlanta rescued her little Chihuahua from the clutches of a coyote." A satisfied smile spreads across Jackson's face. His testimony has been justified. Peace is momentarily restored, but the rumor mill keeps running.

Biddy Pritchett sidles over to Betty and whispers loud enough for hearing aids to squeal. Ruth, who is now settled in a far corner reading *The Charleston Courier,* listens. "I heard by the grapevine that Ruth Smith is writing scandalous things about us here at Sunny Acres. I think a group of us should go to Mr. Capers and complain. She is accusing us of doing nothing except sitting around making up lies about each other. I can tell you right now, if she uses my name in print, I'm going to sue her for all she's worth."

"Biddy, Ruth is the last person who would embarrass anyone. She is writing fiction. Her character in her novel who spreads gossip is imaginary—fictitious. Nobody in Sunny Acres is that evil." A mischievous gleam in Betty's eye is not detected by Biddy's bifocals. A former librarian, Betty Keaton knows how to quell idle talk. At the same time she enjoys Biddy's little tidbits but tries to set her straight when what she says is untrue or malicious.

Dissatisfied with the lack of support, Biddy asks slyly, "Well, how are you and the good doctor getting along? I see you eating with him every night. Any wedding bells yet? Oh, don't misunderstand me; I think it's fine if you can find someone you like to be with. Now me, I have never gotten over Pauli's death. I could never look at another man. His memory is just too precious to me. It's all right for anyone else but not for me. My Pauli treated me like a baby. Brought a cup of coffee to our bed every morning of our marriage. I never worked a day after he married me. He believed a woman's place was in the home. And he left me well-provided for."

Ruth smiles. She is so tempted to ask how much the alimony was when he divorced her for his little secretary who was the brains behind his automobile business. She has had no coffee in bed for over thirty years. What a shame! And such loyalty still. Poor Biddy. Yep! Biddy has reason to be afraid of Ruth's pen. She knows that the second Mrs. Pritchett is a cousin of Ida, Ruth's college mate. Because Alzheimer's has erased Ida's memory and therefore closed her lips, Biddy should feel safe. Ruth's eyes gleam wickedly.

Betty's soft voice, slightly traced with anger, interrupts Ruth's reverie. "I tell you what, Biddy. You will be the first person at Sunny Acres to hear a wedding bell." Betty rises, picks up her coffee mug, places it on the counter and ambles out. In the corner Ruth hides her laughter behind the obituary column in the *Courier*.

Betty's having given his coyote story credence, Jackson has also a little grist from the mill. He picks up the coffee pot and refills his mug. Three packets of Equal dissolve in his brew to which he has generously added cream. Turning to his audience, he asks, "Heard about Richard Capers' first day as CEO?"

Ruth is all ears. She lowers her paper and gives the reporter her full attention. "Well, some woman from the Arbor, I forget her name, was in the beauty salon with her caretaker. When the operator tried to put the woman's head in the washbowl, she began screaming. 'I don't want any water on my head. It is not dirty. It will just wash off my hair color. I can't afford a dye job every week. It's these damn democrats. They want to take all my hard-earned savings and give it to good-for-nothings who won't work.' After her spiel, everybody tries to calm her down including the new CEO who happens to be passing by." Jackson takes a swallow of his brew, stirs in another Equal, and surveys his animated audience.

"Well, you know Rich is a registered nurse as well. So he practices his bedside manner. 'Now, my dear, listen to me. I am Rich. I'm here to help you. A little water, not a whole lot—'

Then the woman screams, 'Rich! If you are rich, you the only son of a bitch here who is.'"

Along with the others, Ruth chuckles, and she reaches for her notebook. At that moment the maintenance manager, Arnold Wiley, rushes into the room.

"I know this can't be true. But somebody just told me that a coyote has attacked one of our residents," Arnold says. Laughter rattles the coffee cups and Jackson is center stage once more.

"Calm down, Arnold," Jackson says. "You talking about Betty's sister's Chihuahua. Her sister lives in

Atlanta. But matter of fact, I did see a real live coyote near the pond this morning."

"Boo!" booms Harry. "He's from Texas. That's not the biggest state anymore, but Texans sure can tell the biggest stories."

Ruth picks up her paper and notebook and heads to her PC. At that moment little Ashley Wilkins comes through the door. Ashley is a petite brunette with a soft voice. She is the quintessence of southern ladyship. Neither indelicacies nor malign gossip escapes her patrician lips.

Biddy looks at her and decides that Weinberg, Mississippi, her hometown, has certainly bred some strange people. Maybe it's what they eat over there. Too much grits and fatback. Doesn't talk much. So Biddy is quite surprised when Ashley makes her announcement.

"I have had the most terrible experience. I was in a hurry to get to my doctor's appointment. I honestly did not see the red light. Then all of a sudden I hear this siren. I thought it was an ambulance taking somebody to the hospital. I even thought it might be somebody from Sunny Acres. So I moved over to the right lane to let the ambulance get by. Guess what."

"A cop on your tail," Wiley offers.

"Pulled right in front of me with that terrible noise and those blue lights flashing. Nearly scared me to death. If my brakes hadn't been good, I would have run into his backside." Biddy titters. "I mean the police car, of course." The look Ashley gives Biddy has lost its Southern reserve.

"What happened, Ashley? Did he give you a ticket?" asks Arnold.

"Well, it was the funniest thing. At least it was to him. I couldn't see anything for him to laugh at. I told him I had a doctor's appointment and just didn't see the red light. And he asked me for my insurance company and I couldn't think of it, because when I changed purses, I must have dropped my insurance card. I told him that Mr. Thomas was my agent in Weinberg. He didn't seem to want to call him and he had a cell phone right there. I could have given him the number, because his wife and I have played bridge every Thursday for forty years except when she was in the hospital having her gall bladder out. That is, when I was living in Mississippi. And you know he just laughed at me as if he thought I was making it all up. It's good I had my driving license with me, or I don't know what would have happened." She reaches in her purse and pulls out a paper. "It's a warning."

"Well, ain't you lucky!" Biddy doesn't ordinarily use slang but the occasion seems appropriate.

"Well, I almost had to go to court. He first said I would have to be in court at nine o'clock on a Monday morning two months from now. I just kinda shook my head. And then the policeman looked at me kinda strange-like and asked what the matter was. And then I told him that I don't get up until ten except when it is something special like a doctor's appointment. Well, he just burst out laughing as if I had said something funny. Then he tore up the ticket and gave me this warning. You reckon there's something wrong with him? You suppose I should call the police department? I heard him laughing all the way to his car."

"I don't think I would do that, Ashley. Some people laugh at the strangest things," Ruth adds.

RICHARD

It is Friday. The last day of school, the paper says. The first of June used to be a joyful time for teachers, especially for English teachers. No essays to grade for two and a half months. Summertime was travel time, reading time, sleeping time, lazy time. Now every day is lazy time in Sunny Acres. Today is Alma time. Alma is the housekeeper who comes every Friday promptly at eight. She likes to have the apartment to herself. Ruth has great admiration for her. She is a single mother who has put two children through college. On a strict schedule, Alma has little time for chit-chat. So after good morning pleasantries, Ruth and Othello settle down comfortably on the patio. With her feet on the ottoman and her computer resting on her lap, Ruth raises the cover and stares momentarily at the keyboard. "Come on, Ruth," she mutters to no one.

"Make your fingers do the talking." Othello looks at her questionably. Is she talking to him? He decides she is in one of those "people moods" that excludes canines. No worry. He can amuse himself and trots off to bark "I dare you" to a lawn maintenance person who is using a blower to clear the wilted azalea blooms. Othello will courageously guard his home and his mistress so long as the intruder keeps a safe distance. Only when he gets closer will Othello fly up the walk and continue his warning in sharp yelps within the security of the patio. "I should have named you Falstaff," Ruth tells him. *"Discretion is the better part of valor,"* Ruth says, quoting the bard's fat coward. Now the blower is close. Othello crouches behind her chair. She smiles at him, waves at the workman and places her fingers on the waiting keyboard. *Once upon a time . . .*

Once there was someone special. John now lies in a little country churchyard in the North Georgia mountains. Once upon a time he was a little boy who picked up windfall apples in those mountains for his grandmother to make a pie. The man he became still loved those mountains as he had loved many things—a doctor who loved art almost as much as he loved science. He thought the human anatomy quite beautiful. Because he loved her, he thought her beautiful, too. She shakes herself and depresses the backspace to erase. "That was a long time ago. Today is today. I must get on with *Sunny Acres,*" she says to Othello and pats his head.

A figure emerges from the gazebo which stands among the trees. Now on the edge of summer, Boston ferns festoon the white octagon and conceal whoever might have been sitting on one of the benches provided for birdwatchers or silent meditators. Richard Blair approaches. He certainly has made a rapid recovery from hip surgery. He walks toward Ruth with no perceptible limp.

"Writing, Ruth? I don't want to interfere with the muse." Othello noses his trouser leg and smells his cat, Cassandra. He knows he has a friend in Richard.

"I'm glad for the distraction, Dick. This is one of those days when the muse is hiding. I find myself in a maze of the past. Anyway, there are enough books in this world already to instruct, amuse, or confuse. As we southerners are wont to say, 'Sit a spell and chew a rag.'"

"My God, Ruth! Where in the world did such English originate? I've been here five years and I still can't sort out what Dixie is all about."

"I can't understand cockney either. Just between you and me, when you Brits talk fast, I can't follow you."

"Well, it doesn't really matter. Just so long as you don't say *just between you and I.*"

"I know what you mean. I don't correct people anymore. Only my enemies, that is. What have you been reading lately?"

"I picked up a little book in our library, *Two Rivers.* It's written by some southern writer. I can't remember

her name," he says, with a twinkle in his eye. Then he
continues, "Anyway, it gave me practice in translating
the vernacular into English. Book was not too bad.
Miss Gurtha, the spinster schoolmarm, took me back
to my school days. My Miss Gurtha though, was not
underweight. You'd think that a Latin teacher would
have *that lean and hungry look* that Shakespeare's Cassius
wore. Not Penelope. That's what we called her behind
her back. She was waiting for her Ulysses to appear.
He didn't. It might have had something to do with her
girth which she stuffed into a staved corset." Suddenly
laughter shook him. "I'll never forget the day when her
knickers fell to her feet. She evidently wore them over
her corset and was unaware that the drawstring had
broken. We were in the middle of Caesar's Gallic Wars,
but Penelope never missed a beat. She calmly stepped
out of her drawers, tucked them under a free arm and
continued. Nobody laughed."

"Poor Penelope!"

"Poor Penelope, my eye. That sadist would assign
half of Virgil's *Eclogues* over holidays. Instead of having
snow ball fights on Boxing Day, we were fighting Virgil
or some other Roman."

"Is that the reason you collected old editions of
Latin texts? You said you had shelves of ancient tomes
under glass."

"Yes, indeed." He is suddenly serious. "Thing is,
we don't give proper credit until later. And you just
listened to me laughing about Penelope and dropping

her drawers. I learned Italian with her and read Dante. She led Virgil and me right up to the gates of paradise. She talked about Dante in exile. Sometime she would get more personal and seem a bit nostalgic. She might comment, 'You know, boys, you will also find that at times life will seem unfair.' Her eyes would have a faraway look. What did we boys know about such dire prognostications? Unfair to us was sitting in a classroom where we could see out the window a cricket game beginning. But I didn't stop by to philosophize. *Well, that was another country,*" he smiles as he quotes Marlowe. Lately the two of them had been playing the quoting game when the two chanced to meet. "My quotes for today," he says. "Your turn. Anyway, I came to make you a proposition."

Ruth lifts her eyebrows in mock shock. "Really, Richard?"

"Oh, nothing indelicate meant! Not to a southern lady. Just an innocent invitation."

"Au shucks," she laughs.

"I wonder if you would join Betty, George, and me for dinner sometime soon. I'll offer you a cuppa or something stronger in my flat before dinner. You know how everybody is wagging about Betty and George. I thought we could give them another wag. Especially if you put an arm around an old codger who has just had hip surgery and look adoringly up into his bifocals."

"Would a little kiss on the cheek make the dog wag his tail more?"

"On the lips would be better. Well, I'll be a son of a gun. The lady is actually blushing." Mischievous glints play in his blue eyes. "Don't worry, my dear. My Don Juan days are over. Who was it who said, "*In the spring a young man's fancy lightly turns to thoughts of love*"? The poet didn't mention an old man though, did he?"

"You forgot, Dick. It was my turn to quote. And oh, you're making my heart go pitter patter. That was Shelley, wasn't it? I would be delighted to join you. Cheers at six?"

"Cheers around five. Bourbon, scotch, or gin?"

"Bourbon. We'uns in the South take it in branch water."

He turns to go but stoops to pluck one of the tulips now past its prime. Holding it up, he says: "*Not the beauty of tulips/nor the taste of mint juleps/ Can compare with your two lips, my beautiful Ruth.*" He bows mockingly and turns homeward. "I'll give you a call as soon as I talk with George and Betty."

"Hey, who wrote those marvelous lines?"

"Hell, if I know. Who cares."

She smiles and thinks of someone long ago who quoted poetry—who found beauty in the spoken and written word as well as the anatomy. And that, too, she thinks, was in another country. She closes the computer and calls to Othello. "Come on, Honey Bunch. I think Alma has finished. I have to wash my hair. I need a new manicure, too."

Yet she does not move. She taps her fingers lightly on the closed computer and watches a hummingbird swoop down to sample the sugared water in the red feeder. He is the first she has seen this year. She wonders if he remembers her patio from last year. Is he again seeking the nectar she has prepared for him? How far has he traveled? His season here will also come to an end. In the meantime, he will make the most of each day. "And so will we at Sunny Acres," she whispers. "And so will I."

THE GOOD SAMARITAN

For those northerners who have come south to escape snow and sleet, Sunny Acres is not disappointing. A hard freeze is rare and snow is even rarer. Summer, however, is a different story. The thermometer hovers around a hundred and residents walk outside either early morning or near darkness. Ruth's Othello grows accustomed to early risings and jaunts around the campus. Vinca, begonias, coleus and other plants hardy enough to resist the heat stand sprightly in glorious array in well-kept beds. Ruth and Othello stroll along enjoying their splendor as well as early morning bird calls. On such a day they walk by the nursing center and watch an ambulance pull up to the front door and unload a passenger. A bit curious like Biddy but concerned that one of the Sunny Acres residents has suffered a mishap, Ruth lingers on the sidelines until she knows that she cannot identify the new face. However, there is something arresting about the newcomer. As the stretcher rolls by, great dark eyes sweep the surroundings. Sharp as a camera's lens, they for a moment focus on Ruth, as if they are adding a new snapshot to an album. Ruth has the uncomfortable feeling that somehow her privacy has been invaded. Then there is the voice. As the newcomer thanks the attendant who adjusts her pillow, Ruth listens to a rather strange mixture of an English accent with a hint of a southern drawl. Might be a story there for *Sunny Acres*, Ruth thinks. I'll definitely pay her a welcome visit.

Waiting a week for the newcomer to get settled, Ruth sallies forth one afternoon to meet the dark eyes. A slim woman wearing a colorful caftan sits in a motorized chair. She has short gray hair that bears the signs of having recently been set. The dark eyes rest on Ruth's face but register no surprise; it is as though she has been expecting Ruth to visit.

"Good afternoon, Muriel. It's all right to call you Muriel, isn't it? Sunny Acres is not very formal. The philosophy is to get to know each other fast and become part of the family. It's Townshend, isn't it? I'm Ruth Smith. I just wanted to drop by, say hello, and welcome you aboard."

Muriel's dark eyes twinkle. "Well, Ruth, when are we sailing? I hope when we get to port, I shall be out of this chair and can throw this oxygen into the ocean."

"If only Sunny Acres were a ship. We could sail right out of here to a cooler climate. Summers in the South are deadly. I remember wearing a coat in July when I was in England. Anyway, welcome to the home of the geriatrics. A few of us take cruises, some walk without aid, some totter along dependent on canes, and some ride their scooters at breakneck speed ignoring any of our more mobile population who obstruct their course."

"And some of us sit in chairs until therapy time," Muriel adds. A wide smile spreads across her olive-skinned face as laughter lights the dark eyes. "Well, it does get hot but it rains every day. I don't suppose there is any perfect place. But how did you know I was English?"

"Actually I saw and heard you when you arrived. There is no mistaking that accent. And I must admit I did a background check. You see, I'm terribly nosy. I'm writing a book about Sunny Acres and just thought you might be an interesting addition. Oh, and by the way, we have one Englishman here, Richard Blair. I'm just getting to know him. He's quite a character."

"Well, I'm sure he is much more interesting than I, especially since I have been reduced to a robot at the mercy of machines. Oxygen, earplugs, and even an electric chair. But a part of me is still human. I love books and used to read voraciously."

Ruth answers eagerly, "I think I was born with a book in my hands. I see you have books." Then she glances at the paperbacks on the bedside table. They don't look like the kind at her own bedside. She decides not to question Muriel's taste.

"Eyes and ears have failed me, Ruth. I am a fit member of the House of Geriatrics. Why do you suppose Browning wrote that old age was the best time of life?"

"He was a writer with imagination. Or perhaps he was oblivious that he had grown senile. Age has turned down the volume in my ears, too, but I thank heavens my eyes are still sharp. And Muriel, I would love to read to you. What about one of those paperbacks?" Ruth picks up one of them. *Daystar's Dilemma.* "Helen Hole. I don't recognize the author."

"You wouldn't. She's not in the literary canon. That is probably a pseudonym. Airport reading. You wouldn't care for her." A mischievous smiled plays on her lips.

"That doesn't matter, Muriel. I suppose I love the sound of my voice regardless of the subject matter."

Now a twinkle invades brooding dark eyes. "Then I would love for you to 'lend to the rhyme of the poet, the beauty of thy voice.'"

"I see you know Longfellow. I believe that came from 'The Day is Done.'"

"Oh, something some English teacher made me memorize years ago," she says carelessly. "Anyway, life is not always poetry. I don't read the heavies anymore. I escape with the Harlequins." The great dark eyes study the glass she is holding as if she were pondering things past. Silently Ruth wonders. *How can Muriel read that garbage when she can quote poetry?* Puzzled, Ruth picks up the book and peruses its cover.

"Do you want to tell me a bit about yourself? We Southerners are very interested in people. We think there is always the possibility of finding in a newcomer a fifth cousin twice removed. Of course, that opens up our chance to put our bit in. No one can stop a Southerner from going into his genealogy—part authentic but mostly hearsay. We actually have a resident here who boasts that she is a direct descendent of Elizabeth the First." They both chuckle.

"Well, as you have so aptly identified, I am English. Actually, I have dual citizenship—born American with acquired English. Like T.S. Eliot, you know."

"Except T.S. revoked his place of birth. He ended up with those High Anglicans. From what I have read of him his personality was a match for High Church ritual." Ruth laughs. "Do you like him, Muriel?"

"I think Ezra Pound is a greater writer."

"Many think it was Pound who shaped *The Wasteland*. Scholarship has it that Pound edited it down to the amazing poem we have today. But look, Muriel, what we have done. We're not sharing the stories of our lives but already have found something in common—poetry. It's a good way to get acquainted, don't you think?"

Her dark eyes focus on the book Ruth is holding. Another flash of mischief twinkles. "Well, let's let

Pound and Eliot rest in peace and turn to a writer who tripled her revenue in publishing. Perhaps Helen is a bit extravagant in plot and style, but she knows what the masses are reading. I find her amusing."

"Well, I should study her style. My literary efforts have not made me rich. So here goes. Chapter One," says Ruth, and she begins to read.

Daystar was given a poetic name because her mother loved poetry. Besides, it rhymed with 'bar,' the place in which she made her hurried appearance just before the break of day on January one. Her mother, Columbine, who read the astrology guide daily and who played the Ouija board, had predicted that the birth would have that setting and that it would be on New Year's Day. The birth was announced to the patrons of Sam Snort's Bar, awakening them from a snooze. The event called for a fresh round of cheer, a little of which was raised to the new mother's lips.

Ruth glances at Muriel and finds her smiling. "Well, this Helen Hole knows how to grab her readers," Ruth says and then starts the next paragraph.

So begins the weekly readings which Ruth discovers she enjoys despite what she considers the "sentimental slop" of the text. In fact, it really is amusing, and her rapt listener never takes her eyes from Ruth's face. Strangely enough, Muriel talks little about herself. She mentions that she worked for a newspaper but doesn't give it a name. Ruth picks up that she has been married, but Muriel speaks of no children. What she does reveal is that she has read widely but seems uninterested in discussing her personal life. At times, Ruth has the feeling that Muriel is playing some sort of game with her. Well, two can play the same game. Their time together is pleasurable but impersonal.

On a hot, humid day in late July, Ruth comes for another session. As she enters the room, Ruth senses a change. The dark eyes are expressionless. Muriel is wearing a robe. On previous visits she was always duly dressed. The welcome that Ruth has enjoyed has lost exuberance, and Muriel's breathing seems labored. Nevertheless, Ruth chirps cheerily.

"Hi, Muriel! How goes it? Are you ready to find out what happens when Daystar finds out that her new husband has fathered a grandchild right under the same roof where the two of them had been enjoying conjugal rights for two years? I'm telling you the writer of this book can really keep a plot skipping."

"It's good to see you." Her voice is scarcely audible. "I know you don't care for these sensational stories. Actually, I don't care what you read. For that matter you could be reading the *Oxford English Dictionary*. I just like company." The voice is breathy. She reaches over to adjust the oxygen. Now the blips are almost constant. A monitor on a pole stands nearby and records numbers which Ruth does not know how to interpret. Still Muriel continues haltingly.

"To tell you the truth, I am more amused by your southern rendition of a salacious love scene. You see, Ruth, I just like having you visit me. Time crawls by. When you come by, I can forget for an hour just listening to your voice. I know I look terrible. Today has not been good. I shall feel better now that you're here."

Ruth pulls up a chair close. Muriel hands her a transmitter attached to a black cord. Today Muriel has both ears plugged with earphones. But despite the artificial devices, remnants of Muriel's beauty remain. A soft pink outlines her smile. The drawl in her voice is more pronounced, sounding more natural than the British accent. Slender hands, knobbed with arthritis, finger the tassels of the afghan that lies across her lap. Visiting Muriel has been such a pleasure. She is pleased that Muriel has also enjoyed the visits. How lonely it must be for only bleeps from the oxygen to keep her company. Ruth wonders what those dark eyes have seen in the past; whose hands have her hands touched. Why has Muriel been so evasive about her past? For that matter neither of them has divulged much about life prior to Sunny Acres. Well, it may be it is time to break the ice.

"Why don't we talk a bit today?" Ruth begins. "I don't know a lot about you. Sounds to me like that with you cutting off those final r's, you and I may be kin in the Low Country. I think you have worked on those final syllables just as I have. As an English teacher, I couldn't be going around saying 'shut de do cause we got to go roun de coner.'"

Muriel smiles. "I wondered how long it would take a writer to admit that she was born in the swamps of the South Carolina Low Country."

"Lawd how mercy. Here I've been reading to you, clipping word endings and putting on my fake Oxford accent. Comes from long practice in the classroom. But I love the soft southern dialect. I'll take it any day to that Brooklyn brogue."

"Have you ever heard of Hellhole Swamp?"

"Hellhole Swamp? You mean Moncks Corner in Berkley County?" Ruth asks with great surprise.

"Sure as shooten. And I mean shooting. You know the story. As people used to say, 'No Negroes after sundown.' Except the N word would be used. Is the KKK still there parading on Saturday nights?"

"How in the world do you know about Hellhole?" Ruth asks with surprise.

Muriel's answer comes in halting staccato sentences.

"I used to live there. When I was a little girl. My mom was a mixture of Cherokee, Negro, white. My dad taught math. In the high school until the Board of Education discovered people of color visiting us holidays. I was twelve. Dad got a job in Detroit. Went on to get a Ph.D. in education. My mom went to graduate school. Taught Shakespeare in a community college." A raucous cough shakes her. She reaches for a tissue and for a minute or so stops talking. Her eyes fasten on the window as though she is searching for some expected caller. "Too many years smoking," she continues. "I lucked into a scholarship to Oxford. Fell in love. Stayed. Mom and Dad retired. They came to me."

"Why did you come back, Muriel?"

"You must know why. I had to come back. Come to terms with the past. Closure. Catharsis." Now she turns and looks directly at Ruth. "I found the old school house where dad taught. It is a community house now. I fell on the steps there. That's where I broke my hip. That's why I'm here."

The door opens. "Did you forget about your therapy, Mrs. Townshend? Sybil is waiting for you." Ruth slips into the hall and watches open-mouthed as the nurse disconnects the oxygen and proceeds to wheel Muriel to the door.

"Sorry about this. I forgot. Let me know when you can read me another chapter. I do know what Daystar's going to do. You see, I wrote the book." The wheelchair heads toward therapy. Muriel turns and bids goodbye in a childlike wave.

"God in heaven!" Ruth sinks into the nearest chair. Now she looks at the author's name. Helen Hole. She grabs her osteoporosis sides to keep her laughter from cracking a rib. Then the sound of Muriel's words sober her. *I had to come back.* Ruth's hand shakes as she opens the book and flips the pages to check the publisher. There is a listing of the novels published. Simon and Schuster. She mutters, "They have not given my work the time of day. Yet Muriel Townshend has made a mint writing twenty-five best sellers issued first in hardback and now in paperback. A take-off on harlequin and chick-lit. Yep! Muriel is wise enough to know that most people are not interested in ideas influenced by Dostoevsky or Kant. Too bad I didn't take advantage of that knowledge. I wouldn't be worrying about the drop in the stock market. Well, the laugh's on me. At least I can laugh at myself. And both of us rooted in the same black soil in the Low Country. God, I can't wait to hear her story."

Two days later the name Muriel Townshend pops out as Ruth does her daily scan of the obituaries in the local paper. Just six lines in the write-up. There is no mention of her as a writer. Services incomplete. There is also the absence of the saccharine "gone to be with God," but there is included that she was born in Moncks Corner, South Carolina, had read English at Oxford and had spent most of her life as a journalist for the London *Times*. No survivors are mentioned.

"My God! What a story! You with your superior intelligence looking down your nose on her tastes. Read English at Oxford. Then why did she resort to writing what was beneath her?" Ruth reaches for her laptop and punches in the London *Times*. Her fingers type out the name: Muriel Townshend. She sees the following article: PROMINET JOURNALIST AND PHILANTHROPIST DIES. *Muriel Morehouse Townshend dies at eighty-five in the States near her South Carolina birthplace. She became a British citizen after receiving an honorary degree from Oxford University, her alma mater. A feature writer for the* Times *for thirty years, in retirement she wrote light romances under the pseudonym*

Helen Hole. The returns from sales she donated to charities including scholarships for minority children. She was preceded in death by her husband, Alexander Fitzhugh, a poet and screen writer for the BBC.

Ruth stares at the screen. A short paragraph speaking volumes. A little black girl from the South who rose from the swamps to become a prominent writer and philanthropist. Ruth picks up the paperback and begins reading about the fortunes of Daystar. As she scans the pages, she follows Daystar, who rids herself of a worthless husband, obtains her GED, and ironically is awarded a scholarship to college by the Daughters of the Confederacy. Her skin is light; the fact that she has one blue eye and one brown eye does not bother her kind benefactors. Neither do they know that her diploma bears the name of Eleanor, her heroine who championed the rights of the underprivileged. Ruth closes the book and places it next to Shakespeare on her bookshelf. Othello tugs the tassel of her robe. It's time for his treat. This morning the pill of liverwurst will be slightly larger because it will be wrapped around his monthly heartworm and flea pill. She reaches down to smooth his little black ears back. "Othello, John would say you look like a bat. That's what he used to call my little dog Puck. But you don't catch bugs, do you? You catch hearts. Just like Daystar." His strident yip moves the treat maker to the refrigerator, and because her mind is on other things, he gets a hefty wad of pâté.

And each man in his time plays many parts. Ruth whispers the words thoughtfully as she snaps the leash on Othello and the two head out for a stroll, with Ruth watching the lights going down on the stage of another act set in Sunny Acres.

THE WAKE

Lord, what fools these mortals be!

Sometime in the night Ruth dreams there is a house—a big house—supported by Corinthian columns with a wide veranda hugging it on three sides. Neither a wicker chair nor a table stands on the marble floor that looks as if it has been recently polished, for the morning sun gleams on its whiteness. The wide oaken door stained in dark walnut is ajar, and Ruth sees down a central hallway that looks as tenantless as the veranda. Suddenly the house rotates three-hundred and sixty degrees and the back of the house is in full view. The back door yawns open. A little light-skinned black girl with pigtails hanging to her waist steps out the door. As she skips along, she does not appear to notice that the house is turning and is now giving her access to the front veranda. Mounting the steps, she ambles toward the open door which closes softly behind her.

A bell is ringing somewhere, but it is the sharp yelp of Othello that transports Ruth from the empty mansion to her bedroom. Sleepy eyes open to a glimmer of sun spreading through the maples outside her window and dappling the lawn in leafy shadows. Othello, her little black clock that never needs winding, announces that it is time to go outside.

Ruth sits on the patio in the cool morning air watching a little black leg poised over a yellow dandelion brave enough to withstand the heat. She contemplates the meaning of her dream. Then Biddy Pritchett interrupts her reverie and Othello's morning ritual.

"Well, blessed if I haven't heard it all now. You know that Anne Byrd. She is having a conniption fit. That stuffed dog of hers that she entered in the live dog show is missing. You know, that stuffed ugly animal with a fancy name. Claims he is her bodyguard."

"Oh, you mean Cerberus. Anne is quite a scholar. She gives all of her stuffed friends classical names. Cerberus has three heads so that his six eyes which guard the gates to hell give him peripheral vision to see that nobody escapes. Anne has a wonderful menagerie. Phoenix, the peacock. Pegasus, a magnificent stallion, Hecate, the big black cat, and—"

"I don't care about those fancy names. It's a shame and disgrace for someone like that woman to live among decent people. If that's education, I'm glad I'm ignorant. She's making a fool of herself over a deformed stuffed animal. And those funny hats she wears. Did you see her last night at supper? She had on a bunny hat, and it isn't even Easter. She belongs in the Arbor along with the other loonies."

Ruth interjects, "You don't mean that, Biddy. Anne is very intelligent. She is an authority on bees and just last week she gave a wonderful lecture on bats. Did you know there is a place in Texas where there is a bat colony that eats thirty thousand pounds of insects in one night? What we need here at Sunny Acres now is a bat house. Mosquitoes love these hot nights. My patio could give them a delicious dinner each evening. Have you ever heard of mosquito a la king?"

Another looney, Biddy thinks. Or maybe Ruth is making fun of her? She thinks she's so smart, because she writes books. She decides that she'll bring Ruth down from that high horse. Her lips curl into a tight smile. Jabbing her cane close to a bed of pink begonias, she smirks, "Well, it takes one to know one. I reckon you love that little black dog of yours more than you do human beings. Me, I try to follow what the bible says and love my neighbor like I love myself."

"Of course, you do, and that's why deep down inside you feel sorry for Anne about her losing her favorite pet. Let's take her some ice cream from the shop. Her favorite is chocolate. That will really cheer her up, especially if you take it. Why just the other day I heard her say that she thought you were one of the best-dressed women in Sunny Acres. She said she was tempted to ask you where you buy your clothes," says Ruth, telling a little white lie. As a peacemaker, she enjoys her little lies.

"Humph! I reckon she spends so much money on those stuffed animals and silly hats that she couldn't afford nice clothes. These trousers came from Pendleton. I paid three hundred dollars for them and this sweater. My mother always told me that first quality always shows. If Anne really wants me to give her a few tips—STOP THAT, YOU LITTLE BLACK DEVIL. Ruth, I do believe he was about to pee on my brand new loafers."

"Come here, Othello. Biddy, he was just being friendly. He probably just smells your cat."

"I don't have cats, dogs, birds or fish! I got more to do with my time than that. I'm the president of the missionary society at my church. We got enough to do to minister to people in need." With that final thrust she turns on her brand new loafers and trots down to share with another resident that Anne Byrd has gone batty and Ruth Smith is not far behind. Othello spins a circle on his hind legs and yips a fond farewell to his retreating guest. The doorbell rings. Othello beats his mistress to the door. There is always a possibility that he can slip out and have a race down the carpeted hallways. This time he is deterred by Anne's Nikes which gently push him inward.

"Hello, Anne. I hear that Cerberus is missing and that you are taking it very hard. Why don't you and Alva come around for a drink tonight? I'll hustle up some vittles in the kitchen. A shot of Jack Daniels will make you remember all the good times you've had with Cerberus."

"Hey! Has Biddy Pritchett been around by chance? I kinda put on a show on the bus last night. You missed it since you decided to skip the concert at St. Luke. Anyway, I truly can't find Cerberus. I think one of my grandchildren may have walked off with him. Well, I went on a crying jag for the ladies on the bus. Alva says I cried real tears, but it was because I was laughing so hard. I decided that Sunny Acres needs a few more laughs after what happened to Carmen. She and her five-carat diamond haven't been seen since she called the policeman a black son of a bitch. Anyway I'm going to have a wake for Cerberus on my patio around five this afternoon. I want to put some invitations in some boxes—including Biddy Pritchett's—and I wanted to see if you could help me with something clever."

"Do you have a black dress? I have a black chiffon scarf with peacocks on it that I bought when I went to see Flannery O'Conner's house in Milledgeville. We could drape it mantilla fashion like a veil."

"I need something to put in people's boxes."

"Well, why don't we do it in a kind of obituary? Let me see. 'Cerberus Byrd, faithful and devoted son of Anne Byrd, has been missing since yesterday. It is believed that he has been kidnapped and probably destroyed, although Anne has received no ransom notice. Friends of Anne are invited to stop by her apartment at five this afternoon for a short service in memory of Cerberus. Please bring your own refreshments, because Anne is an AA member and does not want to risk a relapse.' How does that sound?"

"Ruth, several years ago when I was living in a cottage at Sunny Acres, I lost, supposedly lost, two ducks."

"Real live ducks?"

"No, dead ducks. What in the world would I do with live ducks? You've kept your head in books so long that you are still somewhere up there with some authors, who are all dead, too, like my ducks and Cerberus. Ducks have to have water, silly."

"Well, there's always the bathtub."

"Stop, smart aleck! You want to hear my story?"

"Okay! Shall we name it 'Duck Hunting'?"

"Well, in fact it happened during the duck hunting season. Down here the NRA has a convention in the woods depleting the fowl population."

"How foul! I'm a dyed-in-the-wool Democrat and would like to confiscate every gun in the U.S. and have the guns smelted into cars that run on kudzu."

"Just cause I'm a Republican doesn't mean I don't love animals. If you don't want to hear a good story, that's all right with me."

"Come on, Anne. No politics on this nice morning. As my former maid and good friend used to say— the Good Lord has decided to give us a break in the weather. I'm ready for your ducks. Quack as long as you want. Othello and I have nothing to do until this afternoon when we do dog therapy in Assisted Living. I won't be visiting Muriel Townshend anymore. You know she passed away a couple of days ago."

"Yes, I heard. I didn't really get to know her. She never came to our wine parties on Saturday. You know Alva and I have been pouring wine in the Health Center for years. A couple of Saturdays ago I took my crowing rooster over there and one poor soul was afraid of it. She thought it would nip her. Well, to get back to my mallards. They were kidnapped. At first, I thought the garbage man had inadvertently included them in the morning pick-up. But then I began getting these strange letters. Look here! It's a long tale. Give me five minutes and I'll come down to pick up Cerberus' obituary and show you the clues that led to their recovery."

Ruth smiles. Sunny Acres has its pranksters who bring laughs. It is those kinds of residents who make this life care community feel like not an institution but a home. Like stuffed animals, she muses. Not the real thing but a facsimile. Ruth reaches down and pats Othello's black head. "You are the real thing, aren't you, honey bunch? Somebody's coming. We're going to have more company." Othello perks up his ears and moves his head from side to side. "The Wisdom of

Solomon and the intelligence of Einstein, though you never thought of cutting a baby in two or splitting an atom." Her musings are interrupted by Othello's sharp bark as he tears off across the lawn to meet company. Ruth pulls a chair closer and Anne, her hands holding folders, flops down beside her. She is wearing her red overalls and a yellow shirt ornamented with one of her late husband's bow ties, not black but with a rainbow of colors, a perfect addition to Anne's unique outfit. Othello receives his ceremonial greeting without much ado. Anne is ready to share her story.

"At first, I began getting notes from the ducks themselves. They were written in pencil with the penmanship and spelling of an accelerated kindergartner. Here's one with a duck hiding in canebrake. Read this: *I am scared and lonely. I have lost my clothes. Help me. I may need to buy things. P.S. I am hungry.* And here's one that came by email from <u>The Corporate Chain of Kidnapper and Associates</u>. *If it clucks—we pluck; If it quacks—you'll get it back. www. prank.com.*"

Ruth giggles. "Who in the world was behind this clever nonsense?"

"Our director and her cohorts. One of them was a hunter. Here's how I identified him. I, too, began writing notes and leaving them in places easily accessible to those whom I suspected. Look at this one I dropped in the office box."

Ruth peruses a sheet beginning with 'Tis the pre-season! FOR DUCK HUNTIN. NIGHTMARES ARE GONNA START AFTER THAT FIRST SHOT IS FIRED. BUT MY NIGHTMARES HAVE ALREADY (I WANTED TO USE THE "BEGUN" WORD BUT THE ENDING OF IT {GUN} SHATTERS—AND SOMETIMES EVEN RIPS—MY VERY BEING—SO I RESORT TO STARTED—STARTED. There follows a description of the malevolent duck hunters in blue trucks. The ending was THIS DESPERATE DUCK HUNTER IS ENGAGING IN WHAT HAS BEEN DESCRIBED BY A PRIEST WITHOUT A FROCK AND WITHOUT A FLOCK—"FOUL PLAY."

"What shenanigans did they pull before you retrieved your ducklings?"

"They sent me on all sorts of fruitless hunts including to restaurants, banks, cemeteries—you name it. At last I decided to get into the game and this is the letter I wrote:

My dolling ducks,

I am trying to bare my birdun. Your note of Friday hit me not only in the eyes but between my eyes and stabbed me in left heart. Such news was a terrorbull strain on my scriptural order of casting my birduns. Sunday my lonesome heart fibberlated so bad I had to have a hepper open my letter. But now my birdun seems lighter to see you twogether clothed and looking plump enuff. Watch out for the guidance of that hot mama who has you. I don't approve of you running with the ducks at Westover. With all the sightseeing you doing I scared you gonna end up with bird brains. And stop that snooping! You know what happens to peeking ducks. They end up on menyous. "

"Well, did you ever get them back?"

"One night the special entrée was duck a la anne. Sure enough most of the people at my table ordered duck including me. Halfway through the meal the hostess came to our table and announced that I had a special delivery that required my signature. The security guard at the desk handed me a basket with two ducks perched on a mound of green grass. One had a dunce hat hanging on his bill with a note—It's for the Byrd."

"I bet you wore it."

"Sure did. I came back in the dining room with it perched on my head and with my arms around my ducks."

"What a happy ending! I bet that broke up dinner."

"No, but one of my friends got strangled on a piece of duck and we had to beat her in the back."

Othello surveys his mistress with round black inquiring eyes. His head turns from side to side trying to fathom this seizure that wracks her body. "It's all right, Othello," she says, still laughing, but recovering at last. "Your mama doesn't have epilepsy. It's only Anneitis. Who do you think will come to Cerberus' wake, Anne?"

"All my friends who are all as foolish as I am. They are ready for a few laughs. This hot weather has been getting us all down. Then there are the Biddys who come expecting someone to come to put me in a strait jacket. And then there will be you, looking for another chapter to add to your novel about living in a life care community."

It is a motley crew gathered together to mourn Anne's loss. She is still wearing her red overalls but has added a black baseball cap that tops her short blonde haircut. Curiously enough a gray ponytail has been attached to the back of the cap. Ruth searches for the symbolic significance of the ponytail and decides that perhaps Anne has forgotten that Cerberus is a dog but is making a connection to a horse. It may stand for the famed Pegasus, the flying horse, or it may simply be a sudden inspiration of the creative Anne. Biddy is there in her designer jeans. Richard Blair, who has taken to Anne's wit, is there with George and Betty, the much talked about couple. Richard has finally arranged for the foursome to have dinner together. Ruth smiles at him and thinks an evening with them will be a welcome respite after her grief for Muriel. Many eyes are turned toward George and Betty. Anne, afraid that they will steal the show, begins her eulogy. It, however, is prefaced with her friend, Alva, playing taps on a toy French horn.

Then Anne begins: "Ladies and gentleman, we are gathered here to celebrate the life of Cerberus Byrd. You, who knew him, know that he never spoke an unkind word about anyone. He never broke a law in his life and was a good Republican." Anne pauses while the audience gives a round of applause then continues. "At least he was the last time I saw him. If he by some mistake of St. Pete ended up in hell with all those liberals…." At this point we hear three distinct boos at the most and then she continues again. "He may be a Democrat now, for he was one of those individuals who always wanted to please." Overcome with grief, Alva blows her nose in her tissue and wipes her eyes with her sleeve. "Please, let us not weep for Cerberus. He has gone to a place where there is no discrimination against race, pedigree, or political affiliation. Bless his three-pointed head! He is the peacemaker and is neither gossipy nor mean-spirited. In fact, I can imagine that each of his heads bears a name—Faith, Hope and Love and the greatest of these is—"

Anne is stopped in mid-sentence. In the doorway stands Chester, the beloved staff member and a community volunteer who has been recognized for his service even in Washington. In his arms he holds the lost dog Cerberus, no longer lost and ready to be welcomed by his Sunny Acres family. His mama reaches out to give him a homecoming hug. "Oh, Chester, where did you find him?"

"He was sitting by the pond watching the ducks." Only Ruth hears Cerberus growl, "Lord, what fools these mortals be!"

"WHAT DO YOU READ, MY LORD?"

WORDS, WORDS, WORDS

The beauty salon sits between the assisted living unit and the skilled nursing care area. In fact, there are two salons. The one closer to the Big House, the name for the large building where the independent living apartments are, accommodates the firm. Ruth, when she decides to seek professional care, elects the one farther from her to get the services of the salon serving the infirm. Her preference is both practical and recreational. There is no reason to bother with a hearing aid, for all the patrons are as deaf as she with each voice raised several decibels so that even under the dryer, a listener can continue with the story begun with the shampoo. In addition, Ruth often picks up little tidbits of human interest that may be whipped into a tasty dish for *Sunny Acres* with the recipe for the morsels altered to protect the innocent and the not-so-innocent. The recreational aspect is the opportunity to attend a live soap opera airing such earthshaking phenomena as births of a great-grandson or granddaughter, an anticipated visit or a cruise, the celebration of the ninetieth birthday, the speculation of who is sleeping with whom, or whether the prime rib will be tough or tender. The rumor mill whirls as gray tresses are curled.

There are certain problems involved in getting to the salon. Since there are no traffic directors, one must be wary of the scooter who assumes the speed limit during lunch hour is the same as on the main city highway. There have been broken toes and skinned shins but no fatalities so far. The slower traffic hugs the walls clutching rolling walkers while the more ambulatory wave their canes at the scooters to clear safe passage. Inside, there is the usual scramble for the easiest chair and for possession of the latest edition of the *National Enquirer.*

Violet sits on a high stool attaching thin strands of blonde hair to metal rollers perforated so that the set will dry faster. Her fingers move without her eyes, which are directed at the other operator, Caramel, who is in the middle of telling that someone living on the courtyard has burned up her microwave and smoked her bright yellow kitchen to a dirty gray while trying to cook fatback to flavor collard greens. Several heads have protruded from the dryers to hear the details, but poor Rosie Wakefield, who hears only a jumble of sounds, brays *"WHO, WHO, WHO"* with one hand holding the left lobe of her ear in the direction of the storyteller. Caramel has told this tale a number of times this day, and by this time at least fifteen versions are being shared in Sunny Acres. Ruth hears that the fire has singed Susie McNamara's cat and that the nurse from the clinic has been called to give the arsonist a tranquillizer.

The story comes to an abrupt ending when Violet falls off her stool and lands on her back on the floor along with a tray of permanent wave curlers. Unhurt, she scrambles up and resumes work on her client's hair. By this point Ruth has settled herself in a chair in the corner with a full view of the human menagerie in front of her.

But not for long. Her hair now dry, Dr. Goldstein sidles over and occupies a nearby chair. "Well, what is this hot, dry weather doing to your flowers?"

"I have to water them twice a day. Rain is forecast for tomorrow."

"Well, I'm flying to Denver to see my daughter to escape this heat," Dr. Goldstein replies. What proceeds is a running account of her family who are all members of Mensa. Ruth knows the pattern well. Then follows a travelogue that encompasses both the eastern and western hemispheres, which she enjoyed with her husband. Next comes the solicitation for a contribution to the symphony on whose board she serves. At this point Ruth's mind wanders and picks up what is going on in chair two. There she sees Caramel, a light chocolate African-American woman who has decided that teaching might be a more rewarding career intellectually and financially. She spends her evenings in the classroom pursuing a degree in English and her days in the Sunny Acres rehab center for departing and graying hair. Unfortunately, while exercising her expertise in relating the latest catastrophe, Caramel has inadvertently dropped from one of the sisters of Lady Clairol a red blob on Biddy Pritchett's designer pants. Grabbing the spot remover guaranteed on TV to remove even permanent indigo ink and remembering last night's lecture about Lady Macbeth, she sprays the offending color while orating, "*Out, damned spot! Out, I say!*"

"Caramel, I am a Christian and I don't cuss or allow it around me," Biddy proclaims.

"Oh, I'm so sorry, Mrs. Pritchett. I was just quoting Lady Macbeth, a character we were studying last night in my English class."

"Well, I don't approve of all these bad words writers use in today's books. What kind of clothes was she washing, for heaven's sake, to make her use such bad language?

Smothering a giggle that she camouflages in a cough, Caramel answers. "She had just helped her husband murder the king, and she imagined that some of the blood was still on her hands."

"What is the world coming to when colleges are allowing such murder trash? And all this talk about humans coming from monkeys and denying what the Bible says. The Lord's going to punish us, just like he did the Israelites in the Old Testament. You can take my word for it."

"Yes, ma'am, you probably right. Look, this stuff is magic. The spot is gone. And it only cost $19.95. And you can get two for that price if you order right away."

At this point Ruth is summoned to Caramel's chair while Biddy, swathed in plastic, awaits her transformation from gray hair at the roots to a uniform carrot red. As Ruth is bibbed for washing, she and Caramel exchange smiles, and only at the point that Caramel is rubbing her head in the washbowl does Ruth murmur, *"Out, out, damned spot!"* There follows a conspiratorial giggle. Then Ruth asks, "Caramel, how did you get your name?"

"I know you are thinking it odd that I would be named a color that might evoke racial humor or even slurs. But you know, I like it, even though it has caused laughter. I like it first because of the sound, and I love the way you say it with the second *a*. That way it's poetic—as a dactyl with the accent on the first syllable. And then it even tastes sweet. But the reason my Mama gave me the name is funny. She was pregnant with me and had gained too much weight. Well, her little sister, Florence, had made her first cake under grandma's supervision. It was a three-tiered layer cake sandwiched and marbled with thick caramel. That night Mama ignored the doctor's orders and she stuffed her swollen belly until her palate was satisfied. A few hours later, that night she went to the hospital. My aunt Florence, who connected her cake making with Mama's stomach pain, cried herself to sleep. To make a long story short, I became Caramel and I celebrate my birthday each year with such a cake topped with candles. I lick each one. I can't waste one morsel of its brown goodness."

By this time they have navigated to the chair. Ruth whispers, "Caramel, you talk like an English teacher."

"You mean you're surprised that I know that a dactyl is a foot of poetry—three syllables with the accent on the first syllable."

"Oh, Caramel, I had no intention of offending you."

"I know that Miss Smith. No offense. You see, I read. And I love poetry. And I'm majoring in English. And I don't use such words around here most of the time and risk being called uppity. And one day, like you, I want to write."

"Oh, Caramel, start now. Don't wait until you think you have time. Writing requires craft as well as talent."

"I won the short story contest in high school. I plan to take a course in creative writing next summer. I may need you to critique my assignments."

"Of course, I will. And I know you are a new applicant for a scholarship that Sunny Acres offers."

"Oh, yes. I'm counting on it."

"Listen, Caramel. I have a secret to share with you. You know the lady who recently died here, Muriel Townshend. She was a writer. I didn't know her for very long. But she told me—"

"I know, Miss Smith. She told me, too. She was black but not my color. Born in the South. Her dad married a black teacher. Back in those days couples like that didn't last long."

"How in the world did she happen to confide in you?"

Caramel smiles and says with a wink, "It takes one to know one. Let's get you under the dryer, Miss Smith."

"Call me Ruth, Caramel."

"Okay, Ruth. Only when nobody is around. And I hope your date with Mr. Blair won't be just books." She giggles. "Add a little blush when you make up. Forget your age and remember that first kiss."

"For heaven's sakes, Caramel! Where and when did you find out my having dinner with Dick? I just can't believe this."

"Oh, Mr. Blair's maid is giving him an extra hour so she can polish the silver and set out the hors d'oeuvres. A foursome, I believe. Intellectual compatibility—platonic—isn't that what you white folks call it?"

"What I call it is idle talk for little minds. I'm surprised at your indulging."

"No offense, Miss Smith."

Ruth notes the return of formality, but at the moment she is too annoyed to care. She picks up her purse. "See you later, Caramel. Keep feeding the gossip mill."

In the hall she bumps into Anne Byrd. "Well, who has upset your apple cart? Looks like they've all landed in your cheeks."

"Must be the weather. Where are you headed with that water gun?"

"I thought I would stage a holdup in the beauty salon. Nothing exciting ever happens at Sunny Acres. I thought I'd just enliven the beauty queens."

Ruth finds herself laughing. "What would Sunny Acres do without you, Anne?"

AN OUNCE OF CIVET TO SUMMON UP REMEMBRANCE

Well, what to wear to camouflage the bulge at the waistline. Although Ruth never had Scarlett O'Hara's sixteen-inch girth, she can remember the days when a size eight had just enough roominess that she felt neither fear nor guilt eating chocolate. Snickers candy bars are her favorite. Each gooey, creamy bite melts in the mouth, turning fingers sticky brown until cleaned with the tongue. On her coffee table are three M&M's in a candy dish. Once it had been full in expectation of guests. The three globules left are now brown eyes which follow her each time she crosses the living room. "I will not eat you," she declares as she passes. So she decides that she will let her pale green sweater hang loosely over her white slacks. She spots the glossy green fingernail polish that her great niece left. "Oh, well, what the heck. My nails may add more color to the scenario when the foursome enters the dining room." Waving her gleaming nails in the air to complete the drying, she grabs her purse, and blowing Othello a kiss, she grabs the three M &M's and goes forth.

On the way she meets Anne Byrd, who is entering from the courtyard door. On a satin cushion in a feline stroller sits her tabby cat, Cookie Dough, on her haunches with her paws pushing forward as though she wants her chauffeur to drive faster. "If Cookie were a dog, she would have her tongue hanging out. I have never felt such hot weather," Anne says. A grin stretches all the way across her broad face, and the gleam in her blue eyes spells mischief. She tells Ruth, "I see you are all dressed up for your date." She opens her purse and closes a small package into Ruth's hand. "This is for Dick in case he has none on hand. You can't ever tell about these furriners. Better to be safe than sorry." Her laughter follows her.

"You are a you-know-what—as bad as Biddy Pritchett. The trouble with Sunny Acres is you don't have enough to do or think about. And so you turn an innocent social occasion into salacious gossip."

"Hey! Those frosty green nails are sharp," Anne quips as she swings on down the hall. "I'll bet they'll be the rage of Sunny Acres. Ain't love grand," she trills as she sashays away.

Ruth opens her hand to find a small box of mints and laughs in spite of herself. If people can have a little fun at her expense, then so be it. Sunny Acres is not joyless even though the question *When will it be?* hovers behind doors. When do I step into that *undiscovered country from whose bourn no traveler returns.* Every minute brings us all closer to the end. "Ye gods, I think I need a drink."

When she arrives at her destination, Dick, clad in a burgundy smoking jacket, greets her with a big smile. Behind him sit Betty Keaton and George Clark. For just a moment Ruth studies the pair. Their posture is as formal as the Chippendale sofa upon which they are seated. Although they have played to the Biddy stories, they now find themselves in a social situation where they can be themselves without thinking about the acceleration of gossip. Ruth can imagine the visions of departed Molly lurking behind the forced smiles on their otherwise subdued faces. Molly and Betty had been partners in a dress shop that featured clothes pictured on the pages of *Vanity Fair.* They had been wives of doctors with plenty of free time. The ties became even closer when their children left the nest and George's Pamela married Betty's Gordon. Cancer had broken that circle, first with Tommy and then with Molly, and with that fissure perhaps had come an uncomfortable strangeness. Are they, in truth, considering closing the gap and thus escaping the aloneness of old age? These are Ruth's thoughts as George rises to greet her.

"Well, how is that book coming? Have you already put Betty and me in it? Just remember that a hot water bottle borrowed at midnight has special meaning. A token of affection. A foreshadowing of things to come."

Ruth laughs. "You won't believe this, but years ago in one of my classes we were discussing how fads got started. That was the day of the pet rocks. One of my clever young men said, 'If enough of the right kind of people started wearing hot water bottles around their necks, there would follow such a run on rubber that the price of car tires would double.'"

"And maybe condoms, too," Dick adds. Ruth laughs in spite of herself.

"Aren't you ashamed? I thought Englishmen were trained to keep parlor talk on a higher level," Betty chides.

"Perhaps, but my sainted Catholic mother was French. Despite the disapproval of my staid Anglican father, I learned at ma mere's knee French that did not bear translation into English. For example—"

"That's enough, Dick. Behave yourself. Make the lady a drink," George orders.

The atmosphere of the room has suddenly changed and warmth has invaded the room. Betty and George relax, and Dick hands Ruth a Scotch and soda, saying that his guests are served no bourbon and branch water—the drink of those damn rebels who not only stole English property but also corrupted the language. Ruth tries to think of a sharp retort, but the strains of Beethoven's *Pastorale* emanating from Dick's stereo stop her. It had been their favorite symphony. How many times had she and John listened together, she nestling her head on his shoulder or sometimes each in an easy chair reading a book but with their eyes exchanging contentment in silent communication.

Dick rolls out a trolley filled with a spread that cancels any thoughts of eating in the dining room. "Compliments of our Chef John and Publix grocery," Dick announces.

"Why, Dick, this is a real celebration. What is the occasion?" Betty asks.

"A chance to hear about *Sunny Acres*, to exchange the scuttlebutt heard from the lips of our neighbors, and to get ourselves uproariously drunk." His voice softens, "And to toast those who are here but who are not drinking."

A silence falls upon the room. Ruth feels a guinea-sized egg in her throat. Dick spots the tear wavering in her eye and slips an arm lightly around her waist. Holding his gin and tonic with his other hand, he lifts it with "Cheers! Cheers! Let the party begin."

Ruth settles herself in a wingback chair and surveys the room before her. Does the décor of a room reveal the character of the tenant? Books! Book cases from floor to ceiling holding volumes bound in colorful leather. From her chair the authors are indecipherable, but she could imagine that the rise and fall of Greek and Roman empires are encased between their handsome covers. There is not a single paperback in sight. Not even a copy of her hardback *Two Rivers* to flatter a guest, yet Dick had mentioned that he had read it. Reaching for a cracker topped with brie, she asks, "Dick, I suppose you don't condescend to read paperbacks. Are all of your books first editions? It's a good thing my first book was at least in hard cover; unfortunately, my second one is in trade paperback."

"My dear madam, shall I take you into my bedroom this early in the evening? In addition to an inviting queen-sized bed, you may be surprised what you find on my bookshelves. In fact, I have just reread *Stars over Dixie,* one of Muriel Townshend's romances. I wonder why in the name of heaven she uses a pen name like Helen Hole. Seems to me she would have made the name more interesting if she had used Hell instead of Helen. I asked her that once, but she flashed those big brown eyes and said, 'Dick, do you know how to use the Internet?' She was always good about changing the subject when she didn't care to answer a direct question."

Ruth is speechless. She almost drops her drink in her lap but manages to retrieve it, spilling a few drops on her white slacks. She places the glass on the table beside her and whispers shakily, "Dick, do you mean that you actually knew Muriel Townshend?"

"Of course, I do. What's so strange about that? England is not so large as the States. In fact, she did several pieces for the *Times* on some rare volumes I was able to get. She was interested in early African art, and I directed her to Quagga Book Sellers in South Africa. She and I are casual friends. Casual enough to meet for tea once or twice a year. Not close enough to share Boxing Day."

"Are friends. *Were* friends. Dick, did you know she died here at Sunny Acres last week?"

"You've got to be joking. The Muriel Townshend that I know is probably in her flat in London spinning out another tale about unrequited love."

"No, she isn't, Dick. No, you evidently don't know how to use the Internet. I read the obituary in the *Times*." Ruth's voice quavered. "You see, I read her latest novel, *Daystar's Dilemma,* to her. It was only on the last day of reading that I connected her with the author, Helen Hole. Dick, she was born in the Low Country of South Carolina, near where I was born. The area in Berkley County used to be called Hell Hole Swamp. Part of the population was a gang of rednecks who had no hesitation using the "N" word as they proclaimed proudly, 'Us don't allow any dem folks after sundown.'"

For a few moments no one speaks. It is Betty who breaks the silence. "You remember, George. The nurse asked you to take a look at her before the ambulance came. We happened to be visiting in the area."

"Of course, I remember. She was gone before the paramedics arrived. Quite peacefully, it seemed. I thought at the time how superfluous the oxygen tank was. An author, you say? Born in the South? A British citizen? You knew her, Dick, and didn't even know she was here at Sunny Acres? Why this is fantastic! Unbelievable!"

Richard Blair is visibly shaken. He leans against the walled bookcase, his eyes staring into the distance, his hands mindlessly turning his gin and tonic. "If I had only known. My god, what a woman! She wrote those trashy books to help trashy people. She could have been giving A.S. Byatt a run for her money."

"Not trash, Dick. What you call 'trashy people' were hopeless people who were not privileged to go to Oxford or for that matter to retire in a place like Sunny Acres. You see, she knew bigotry. She could identify with what you might call *trash*. And she knew that trash would sell much faster than books by Byatt and Iris Murdock. She knew that even some Oxford graduates might read her for amusement. She knew the level of most people's tastes. Her interest was not literature but money."

"But why? Surely her family didn't belong to the rednecks you describe. What made her such a humanitarian?"

"No, she was not a redneck. Her father was a principal of the school. But her mother was part black. The discovery cost her father his job."

"In God's name, Ruth, how do you know all this?" Dick's words come quickly, tinged with anger. He has just been reprimanded for being a bigot himself.

"She told me," Ruth answered quietly. "The last time I saw her. I was so looking forward to getting to know her. That didn't happen. I read the obituary in the paper. You see, she was not a resident but was temporary until she got over hip surgery."

"You knew she read English at Oxford?"

"No, Dick. I read that in the *Times,* too. She had a sense of humor and couldn't help telling me that she was the author of *Daystar's Dilemma.* I felt as embarrassed as you did when you called her charity trash. I had been looking down my nose at her with my superior tastes. I'm sorry I jumped on you, Dick. I haven't quite gotten over the experience. And I don't want to. It brings up remembrances of things past. I was a part of her past. Except, unlike her, I have almost forgotten it. But then I didn't have Negro blood," she finished quietly.

"I want another drink," George said. "Let's drink to Molly and Muriel and all the others."

Simultaneously the four rise. Their glasses make faint clinks as they touch. Dick says hoarsely, "Cheers."

"How well did you know her?" Ruth asks cautiously.

"Some day I might tell you. But not tonight." He raises his glass and empties it. Then his arm goes around Ruth's waist. To her surprise, she does not mind at all.

POLITICS

A certain convocation of politic worms...
Hamlet, *Act IV, Scene 3*

Sunny Acres is a diversified community. Although the deep South claims the largest number of residents, records show cross country addresses. A number are naturalized citizens, having come from their homelands seeking better educational and professional opportunities. There are also those who bring with them horrifying stories of tyrannical rule, resulting in enslavement, warfare, and even genocide. In short, Sunny Acres is a melting pot of strong-minded people whose lives and opinions have been shaped by culture, parentage, and education. For the most part, when beliefs clash, the arguments remain civil enough that a Georgia Bulldog fan can still dine amicably with a Florida Gator who has just quelled the bark of a Bulldog for at least another year.

Fall is the season when the spirit is animated even though the sap is not rising. It is the time for games, the time for elections. The end of summer and falling leaves stir memories. Dr. Ellison, for example, remembers the good old University of Georgia days when she led the women's basketball team to victory. She is no less supportive of the football team now. Saturdays are sacred days when neither death nor taxes can separate her from the high definition widescreen box on which she watches the red and black wage battle on the turf. With her are her two fellow fans attired appropriately in their colors and armed with kazoos tooted in victory but sometimes sounding taps for the fallen. Anne, the animal lover whose abode houses a menagerie of stuffed animals, as well as her cat, Cookie Dough, wears a Georgia helmet fashioned in down—the favorite nesting place for Cookie Dough when it is not on Anne's head. The third of the trio, Dr. Alva Faulkner, who dropped only one baby in her fifty-six year practice of obstetrics and who is related by marriage to the Nobelist from Mississippi, is a bit more subdued than her mates, although, she, too, trod the sacred halls of the University of Georgia. Perhaps her animation has been fully spent on new papas to whom she presented all those new bundles of love. She appears to take defeat more calmly. At least she does not don the colors of mourning nor do her lips turn down in a permanent scowl.

Prior to the game this trio parades through the lobby and the dining room with the promising notes of victory predicted in every blast of their kazoos. The horns are so loud that even Ruth wrests from her bad ear the hearing aid there and promptly decides she must make another trip to the audiologist to tone it down. During the game, refs make wrong calls that should have been challenged by the coach. Smiles are now gone from the faithful Bulldog fans. Only on another Saturday might the Dogs once more conquer their foes to bring back the smiles of victory. A walk down any Sunny Acres hall or a glance into the club room will reveal similar groups in huddles watching their alma maters vie for victories and ultimate bowl bids. It is a good time for Sunny Acres when the past is recreated with no memories of pacemakers, knee replacements, nor balding heads.

Somewhere in Sunny Acres there may also be a conclave of Rebels and Yankees who are engaged in that timeless battle between the North and the South. The Mason Dixie line divides the group while a few lookers-on, now labeled as liberals or leftists, sit on the sidelines, having consigned the war to a part of history and caring less whether it is called the Civil War, the Confederate War or the War Between the States. They listen with amusement:

"Those abolitionists just stirred up trouble. In another ten years slavery would have been a thing of the past with the invention of the cotton gin and pickers."

"What amuses me is why this bible-belt South didn't question the morality of it."

"You think that's why you damn Yankees fought? Why even your commander-in-chief said he couldn't give a damn about the war. It was the Union, man. Saving the Union. I heard on the news yesterday that Texas has the right to secede from the Union. Good idea! The Whole South what with the White House and those damn Democrats wanting to socialize us."

"Come on, man. You're just a bad loser. Your bible belt doesn't condone such talk."

"Bible belt, my foot. If I know my history, it was the Puritans who brought in the blue laws. We Southerners came from the aristocracy in England. Church of England. Whiskeypalians. My great grandpappy and Joe Kennedy made a pile during Prohibition."

"Is that why you wanted Ted to be President? Cousins under the skin."

"Come off it. Southerners have respect for the dead regardless of politics. Didn't I just say we came from aristocracy?"

"And some of your aristocrats lived on Tobacco Road?"

"Oh, those people spilled over from the North. Couldn't stand your cold weather."

"Well, my great grandpappy must have been a gentleman, too. Here's his favorite story from World War I. Grandpa was a West Pointer and a Colonel. One day a new volunteer came before his board to apply for OCS. He was a hefty little fellow who had been assigned to the kitchen even though he had a new degree from the University of Georgia. Grandpa had a great sense of humor and enjoyed rankling southerners. 'Soldier,' he asked, 'have you ever heard of a man by the name of Sherman?'

'Yeah, that son of a bitch burned my grandmama's house down,' was the bullet reply.

Unable to suppress his laughter, Grandpa said, 'You'll do. Pass on.'"

There follow general hee-haws. Not to be outdone, the true southerner in the group replies, "I expect you're right. Your grandpappy must have got mixed up and married one of those Yankee girls. Just shows a southerner never forgets his raisings."

"Come on, now. Today is November eleventh. Armistice. I have Jack Daniel waiting for us to sign a treaty." Bothwell Walton has decided that only Jack can close the argument in friendly terms. "Gentlemen and Ladies," says the host raising his glass, "let's drink to Jack, the great arbitrator who knows how to reconcile all differences."

"Then we should save a drop or two for the Georgia fans. Last time I heard, the Gators were taking a bite out of the Dawgs."

"Speaking of d-o-g-s, Ruth, your mutt won Best of Breed, I hear."

"You heard right, Bothwell, and Othello is not a mutt. He is a purebred long coat Chihuahua. His grandpappy won best in show at Madison Square Garden."

"This sounds like Grandpappy Day. One a Yankee colonel who took pity on a poor southern soldier, one an entrepreneur of white lightning during the war when the Yanks beat the Rebels so bad that they couldn't sing 'Dixie' for forty years, and now some judge bribed to give a Mexican half-breed best in the show."

"You're just angry, Bothwell, because my dog beat your King Charles Cavalier. Don't call us Southerners poor losers, and stop bragging about your royal background."

Bothwell's eyes twinkle mischievously. "Seems to me that tongue of yours has been even more tart since you've been taking a nip with Richard Blair. Tell us, Ruth, do you two just talk about books all the time?"

"No, we leave room to get a little grist from the rumor mill, Bothwell. We hear you'll be dancing with Biddy Pritchett in *Bits of Broadway* coming up next week."

"You heard exactly right. Biddy and I are going to show Sunny Acres how to shake a leg. All for a good cause, Ruth. Just like the dog show. Be honest with me, Ruth, how much did you pay the judge for your dog to win?"

"Ten dollars more than you paid him, Bothwell," she retorts, laughing. "You see, it was all for a good cause. Our bribes went to Alzheimer's research."

From down the hall come the sound of hoots from kazoos and a dozen yells, with one clearly rising above the din. "Georgia! Georgia! Georgia!"

MEMOIRS

The Wellness Committee lives and breathes to plan activities for the residents of Sunny Acres to reinvigorate minds, bodies, and souls. One of these progressive planners decides to promote a seven-step program that involves oiling old joints, awakening the intellect, and stirring old memories. Completion of this curriculum results in a graduation with diplomas (not in parchment) and minus caps and gowns. The doctors among our residents insist, however, in a hooding ceremony with a degree in post-graduate geriatrics. One of the requirements is to write a memoir. A number of old eyes sparkle at the thought and fingers begin to scratch heads (some of them almost bald) to revive the past. Many raise questions: "How do I start?" "Do I have to tell the truth?" "How long should it be to get credit?" and "Does the committee have to read it?" Others dismiss such nonsense and return to their bridge tables; some abandon the project immediately, offering their strongest reasons: "I can't remember what happened five minutes ago much less eighty years." "Let bygones be bygones—that's what I say— live today, hope for tomorrow, and forget the past." Such negativity does not deter our bright committee members, who turn their ears toward those writers who are willing to ink their past if they can have a little direction. Ruth Smith is the answer. The committee persuades her to conduct a class on writing memoirs. She sits on her patio and, as of old, begins making mental lesson plans.

Fall seems the season to reflect. Ruth watches the trees as their leaves lazily drop to the lawn still flourishing in spring-like turf. Golden ginkgoes compete with the red dogwood. Right in the middle of scarlet sprawl sits a green limb as though it is protesting change. Ruth has often thought that nature puts on her gorgeous finery just before the *blond assassin* (Dickinson's metaphor for first frost) strikes. Now she ponders a way to tell her class how to record the seasons in color so vivid that great grandchildren can enjoy and relive the past. Ruth has never taught such an esteemed class of pupils, whose degrees outrank hers but whose stories she knows could illuminate her craft. Her mind turns to a former resident, Muriel Townshend. No one had even an inkling that she was a graduate of Oxford, and a noted London journalist who wrote chick lit under a pseudonym. Did she write a memoir? Somewhere there should be the story of young Muriel, whose father was white and mother black, both educators driven from Hell Hole Swamp in South Carolina so nicknamed for its racial prejudice. Now deceased, right here in Sunny Acres, who knows that she had given millions to promote racial understanding from the sale of her novels? Her secret remains secret unless *Sunny Acres* tells it. And what about the others here? Funny Anne, brilliant Dr. Amanda Goldstein, witty Richard (she is developing something for him that she can't quite put a name to), and even Biddy—each is worthy of remembrance. Each could brighten, like the autumn trees before her, a day for somebody in the dim future. She smiles as she scrolls through the pages of *Sunny Acres*.

And now the teacher stands before her new class. Each participant has brought pen and paper to record what Ruth hopes will be inspiration. She launches her lesson with the technicalities and the warnings of turning a great story into mere genealogy. She recommends beginning with the idea of snagging the reader at the outset and reads several passages from authors who have done just that. The night before her lecture, her friend Anne had announced her intention of writing a memoir or a memorial to her animals and shared her beginning during dinner. Ruth had recommended rewriting the opening paragraph about Bubba, the family's beloved dog, who had been rescued from a shelter. "You need snap," Ruth had advised.

Now Anne rises to announce that she is ready to share with her writing class how to get snap in the opening. She steps gingerly into the aisle and faces her fellow writers. "Bubba, too big for the Christmas stocking but eager to show gratitude to his new family who had rescued him from the shelter, bounded into the house and peed on one of the angel ornaments just high enough that his leg could decorate the angel's white satin dress with yellow diamonds." A roar emanates from the class. Richard Blair rises to share his own family genealogy, this one British. He says, "That bloke, Tony Blair of dubious origin, fourth cousin removed from the Prime Minister, fucked my mother on their wedding night as they lay under their bed while bombs rained down from those bloody Germans and so here I am." Mischief dances in his blue eyes as he throws Anne a wicked grin and says, "A Brit can outdo a Reb any day."

"Them's fighting words, Dick!" Anne yells. Dick, ignoring the rebel yell, pretends to read from his beginning memoir. Ruth grabs his blank notepad and shouts above the clapping of eighty hands, "SUNNY ACRES SHALL COME TO ORDER!" The teacher, though convulsed in laughter, is afraid that a profane war of words might begin a battle that will offend the sensibilities of a more genteel group. The continuation of her lecture on the difference between a memoir and an autobiography meets with muffled no's of disappointment. Other salacious examples would be much more fun. She wonders what these budding writers will produce at the next session, and while she is opposed to censorship, she may have to curb some of the enthusiasm by advising a bit of restraint in the choice of words.

Before she can decide the most effective and diplomatic approach to discourage future showoffs, Ashley Wilkins at the back of the room waves a yellow legal pad to get attention. Ruth remembers how Ashley, by gently asserting that her sleep routine could not accommodate a court appearance, talked a traffic cop out of giving her a ticket. Certainly this little lady from the Deep South possesses neither an indelicate nor prurient vocabulary. Ruth raises her hand and nods in her direction. Clutching the shoulder of the man sitting next to her for support, Ashley struggles to her feet, holding on to her manuscript that she apparently wishes to share.

"Now I know that you said that memoirs should be true and this is true, but you see this is a dream I had just last night. You see I dream every night and I dream in Technicolor. I'm an Episcopalian, but I don't go to church often because it's so hard to get up and down with my knees, and I've even had both of them replaced. I was in rehab six weeks for one and three months for the other. That godly priest from Our Redeemer came to see me every day. If anybody goes to heaven he will, even though he is in favor of women preaching, and somebody said he voted for that homosexual bishop, but I don't believe a word of it—why he brought me Holy Communion every Sunday night, and he didn't even want to take the twenty dollars I gave him which he said would help with paying for gas. And course he knows I don't go to church regular, but I try my best to get there Easter and Christmas and on St. Francis' Feast day when I take my precious little Sugar Tit to be blessed." She stops to get her breath and recovers quickly. "I named her that, because when she was just a puppy she would snatch my grandson, Wally Joe's pacifier when he dropped it."

A general titter floats across the room while a couple of men bray loud hee-haws. Unaware that her digression has been amusing, Ashley continues.

"I think it must have been something I ate—maybe what Chef John calls one of those highfalutin names that's really just ordinary vittles like creamed chicken—anyway I dreamed I went to Our Redeemer and took Sugar Tit with me. And it was Easter but it was night because I remember I had to check if I had my parking lights off. That old Chevrolet is fifteen years old and that battery is going any day." She stops again to blow her nose and swallow water from a bottle which she has been carrying in her shoulder bag. "Anyhow, I kinda had Sugartit hiding behind the prayer book because I know not everybody is an animal lover like me. But she was just as good as she could be until the usher passed the collection plate which was full of checks. I don't know what possessed her to snap at Mr. Austin unless she thought he was going to hurt me when he gave that friendly Easter pat on my shoulder, but up she jumped, growling, and her teeth just missed his hand. I was so embarrassed that I grabbed her up and was going to take her out of the church and miss Communion, but then I dropped my pocketbook. I stooped down to pick it up and Sugartit jumped out of my arms. That little devil flew right up to the altar and was about to do number two on the prayer cushion when I caught her and hauled her out of there. I was so relieved when I woke up and knew it was all a dream. In fact, Sugartit was sleeping peacefully on her little blanket at the foot of my bed. Of course, it was just a dream, but it was so real to me that I wondered if I could put it in my memoir."

Richard Blair, who is sitting three rows from the speaker and does not know her name either, jumps to his feet and says solemnly, "Madam, I think it should definitely go into your memoir, but I also think that the good Lord is telling you something in your dream. He's sending you a message that you ought to join the Baptists."

She looks at Richard in complete bewilderment. "Do you really think so?" she asks.

MY DOG FLUSH

Billy Watkins is one of the Sunny Acres residents who is a member of that elite group known as "characters." He lives on the Courtyard three doors down from Ruth with his dog Flush. Preferring his dog's company to that of his neighbors, he is generally considered a loner. Flush, a Schipperke, is a beautiful lady. She belongs to the pedigree of those ancient Belgian barge dogs which are de-tailed shortly after birth. Black as a midnight without moon or stars, Flush has a short porcupine coat which she wears regally as she trots along by her master. How did she ever get the name Flush? Elizabeth Barrett Browning's little spaniel, Flush, the color of ripe wheat, made literary history. She was nestled in a basket and handed over to Robert Barrett Browning as he and Elizabeth and the dog ran away from her possessive Papa. *Flush* rhymes with *blush* which women wear to give pale skin a natural color. Estee Lauder blush would be lost on Flush though her coat has a beautiful sheen. No help there. So why in the world would Billy Watkins name a black canine Flush?

These are Ruth's thoughts as she watches Billy and Flush stroll across the lawn now sprinkled with the last crepe myrtle leaves. As usual, Billy wears overalls, blue-striped with bib and suspenders indigenous to cotton and cornfields rather than an exclusive life care community. It is his daily attire except for Sunday, when Sunny Acres accepts no bearded farmer even near the precincts of its Holy Day Buffet. Once a week Billy molts his feathers and appears in the dining room in a dark blue suit with accessory shirt and tie, clean-shaven and barbered, ready to be photographed for Vanity Fair featuring Armani. Only one aspect of his anachronism remains: his speech. When he opens his mouth even to say "good morning," there is no mistaking that his strange twang comes from a forgotten time buried in the old South. It is also evident that he has gone to school where the verb *to be* was conjugated *I ain't, you ain't, she ain't, we ain't, they ain't.* Strangely enough, his grammar is not offensive to most of Sunny Acres. Only those who don't know the difference between *who* and *whom* mimic him behind his back. Biddy Pritchett is a prime example. But Ruth is not one of these. She watches him this morning as he kneels down to untangle Flush's lead and to brush from his back a clipping pruned from a boxwood. She thinks there is something almost aristocratic in Billy's posture that has nothing to do with his clothes. A story behind every door, she muses. She would like to open that door, but she fears that her reputation as an old maid English teacher, a dyed-in-the-wool grammarian, might deter her entrance. No wonder she is astonished when he turns Flush toward her patio and leads her up the stepping stones to where Ruth sits. Othello rises, but instead of giving his usual growl when another canine invades his domain, he wags his tail. Flush, tailless, eyes Othello with no hostility. It is as though she is saying, "Look, brother, we are the same color and kin through literature."

Billy reaches down and strokes Othello's head. He speaks first: "*I am a man more sinned against than sinning.* Othello, you don't look as though you have done much sinning. I bet you love your mistress as much as the Moor loved Desdemona." His deep, dark eyes search Ruth's reaction. She knows he expects her to register amazement. A country hick quoting Shakespeare. Not Ruth. Instead she remarks blandly, "Indeed, he does, Billy. Perhaps more. Certainly he would never get angry enough to strangle me. His love is unconditional—like God's."

"Ain't no nothing about God. But Flush thinks if there is one, I'm him.—He, if you prefer."

"Not nothing to know, Billy. It's all up here." She taps her head. "Faith is what the preachers call it."

"Well, us humans got to have faith in something. Flush here is good enough for me."

"But don't you think it would be comforting to believe somebody is standing near when the grim reaper comes calling?" Ruth cannot believe that in a few minutes she and Billy Watkins have launched into such serious subjects as life and death.

Billy, uninvited, eases himself into the patio chair across from her. He holds Flush by the leash between his knees. The bank of amber chrysanthemums in a flower stand behind him frames a silver head with no trace of baldness. His brown eyes slightly sunken in their sockets regard her as if he is amused. Ruth wishes that she had a camera—not to show the picture later to provoke laughter—but to study it herself, to seek the mystery behind this face before her. If only her fingers could be the camera! Here is this loner, whose clothes belong to the tobacco fields in the Low Country where she was born, who speaks in a potpourri of poetry and patois.

"Do you realize, Ruth, that so far, with the exception of Richard Blair's graphic depiction of his parents' honeymoon, the memoirs have centered on dogs? To name a couple, there was Anne, I forget the last name—privately I call her 'free spirit'—and Ashley Wilkins—yes, that is her name—the woman whose dog Sugartit almost pooped on a prayer cushion. If I were a better, which I am not, I'd bet Othello here has found his way into many pages of *Sunny Acres*. Right now you are wondering why in God's name—though I have told you I have no acquaintance with the Trinity, Buddha, or Krishna—my girl here is named Flush."

"It would not take a mind reader to know that I'm curious, Billy, but I won't be disappointed if you don't give me Flush's biography. You see, I love mysteries almost as much as I love Shakespeare. So don't feel like you have to share with me why you came to Sunny Acres, or why you have to hide a sheepskin under the garb of a peasant, or why you have named your dog after Mrs. Browning's."

"Flush is the name of my wife. She also loves dogs. She disliked her own name, Mary Grace, and renamed herself Flush after I told her the Browning love story on our honeymoon. She murders the King's English now. Once she, too, knew the difference between *he* and *him,* but she has reverted to her sharecropper background. Neither case nor subject-verb agreement matters to her now. I don't matter either. In fact, she recognizes me only when I go to see her dressed like this. Sometimes, even then, she looks at me as if I were a stranger. She might say, 'You ain't heard nothing from William, is you?' I don't tell her that William is dead. She would give me an argument."

"Billy, who is William?"

"He was our son."

"What happened to him?" Ruth whispers.

"Flush, his mother, killed him."

SUNDAY AT SUNNY ACRES

At Sunny Acres, every day is Sunday. Nobody thinks about going to work the next day, hassling with a boss, making an executive decision that will make employees enemies, rising and shining for Uncle Sam's roll call, giving a paper a "D" that deserves an "F," or playing host or hostess to fifty people who are absolutely the dullest humans alive. Yet according to the calendar, the seventh day that the Lord has made does roll around, and momentous decisions must be made.

The church-goers fall into certain categories: barring calamity and catastrophe, the devout will don their Sabbath wear, place their bibles in zippered cases, and either take advantage of waiting buses or use their own vehicles to chariot them to the worship places of their choice. The Jewish population, most having celebrated or not celebrated Sabbath the previous day, are left to their own devices. Another group, not quite so devout, will decide that the pain in the pelvis is a bit too severe to sit in St. Paul's uncushioned pews; still another is the group that thinks like Emily Dickinson about the Sabbath: *"I keep it, staying at Home."* They may take a walk around Sunny Acres and listen to the choirs of nature sing hallelujahs to the skies. Of course, there are the unbelievers who may join the Sunday walkers or find other diversions in such places as *The New York Times,* a favorite CD, or a trip with Google to exotic shores far, far away from life care communities. Those who are not ambulatory may seek comfort in a televised sermon, visit neighbors, or wheel themselves abroad down the byways of Sunny Acres' long halls. Ruth Smith, having decided to skip an unorganized sermon on the sins of the flesh and godless Democrats, decides to join the Sunday strollers.

November in the South can be very pleasant. Although only a few leaves cling to the trees, frost has not touched Ruth's patio garden. Two and three feet high, the coleus have outlasted summer heat and still display color that rivals any autumn trees. Occasionally a stroll requires a sweater, but today nature has smiled on Sunny Acres, inviting walkers to take advantage of its clemency. Winter is drawing near. A light wind lifts

Ruth's hair and bars momentarily her vision of the floral hexagon of pansies at the front entrance. She brushes the wisps from her eyes and jumps as Richard Blair touches her arm.

"Well, old girl, playing hooky on the Sabbath? What will St. Peter say?"

"Undoubtedly what he has been saying to you for years. I bet you're not even an Easter or Christmas churchman."

"Wrong about that. I loved the ritual of high mass. I even tutored Muriel Townshend through a Christmas Eve service at St. Paul's. The restoration had just been completed. You said you saw what a wreck it was. St. Paul has been cursing those damn Krauts ever since. They almost demolished it."

"Stop cursing the Germans, Dick. The war is over. That's what I keep telling southern rebs. As Lady Macbeth said, *What's done is done.*"

"Neither you nor Lady Macbeth lived through the blitz. Muriel Townshend and I did."

"Tell me more about her. How did you meet?" Ruth steers him toward an empty bench where she sits. "Sit down for a spell."

"What do you want me to say? Wicked words about Muriel and me that you will transfer to your laptop? Or is there a chance you could be a bit jealous?" Ruth ignores the last remark.

"Oh, no! I am deeply offended. I am not Biddy Pritchett."

"*No offense i' th' world*," he says, smiling as he sits down. "Actually there is nothing to tell. Both of us were bibliophiles. I made lean living selling rare books. She made a fortune writing trashy ones. Say now, did you recognize my quote?"

"Of course! *Hamlet*. I had a dog named Hamlet once. In fact, he preceded Othello."

"You also had someone who used to read *Hamlet* with you,"

Ruth turns sharply. "How do you know that?"

"As your Ben Franklin so aptly put it, 'Three can keep a secret if two are dead.' What happened, Ruth?"

"To quote you, actually there is nothing to tell. Both of us were bibliophiles. He was a doctor who thought human anatomy as beautiful as Shakespeare. I was a teacher who thought his simile inappropriate."

Dick smiles roguishly. "I have no laptop to record romances, but like the cat I am curious."

"You know what happened to the cat? Curiosity killed him."

"Then like a wise cat, I shall ask no further questions."

"Well, you can be a good boy at times." She smiles and takes his hand.

"You know, Ruth, I do read rather well. Better than Olivier, but then he was a good-looking scamp. Would you be willing to give me a try-out? It would be fun, don't you think?"

"You know a new play-reading group has just been formed at Sunny Acres. Perhaps we could suggest a *Hamlet* read."

"I had imagined something more intimate." He raises her left hand and thumbs the diamonds on her fourth finger. He is about to say something when Billy Watkins appears in his Sunday best.

"Morning!" Ruth is so grateful for the interruption that she gives Billy her broadest smile.

"Where is Flush?" she asks.

"Which one, Ruth?"

"Is there more than one, mate?" Dick asks.

"I left Flush, my dog, reading Browning. I don't know what my wife, Flush, is doing." With that Billy waves goodbye and strolls on.

"What a sense of humor!" Dick laughs. "I sometimes think this place is just another Bedlam. I heard about the lady escaping the Arbor to get to her wedding."

"I see no cause for laughter, Mr. Blair. Such aberrations are not funny. Besides, you don't know the truth behind Billy's words." Strangeness begins to creep in between them.

"No offense, Ruth. Sometime laughter is the only avenue to escape. A brittle tongue may be just another way to screen pain. It may be that Billy Watkins' peculiar transformation on Sunday is just a shield. It's to protect him from what he perceives is real danger should someone attempt to crack his armor. Who has peeled Biddy Pritchett's carapace? Who wants to? Why has she made herself so forbidding? It may be that the lady in the Arbor is the lucky one. If she never gets to her wedding, she will always have the anticipation of arriving. And your friend, Ida. She will always be looking forward to going home to her little house." Dick stops speaking as they move toward the entrance. Silence walks between them. Then he continues softly. "You must admit that life here is somewhat strange. We have all come to spend our last days here for the modicum of security that Sunny Acres offers. I don't disparage the excellent care nor the beauty of the grounds. But to a large extent, we live as strangers. Breaking down barriers is very risky. There is always the fear of betrayal. There are some of us," he says slowly, "who are not so fearful. I am willing to take risks. You know George and Betty are about to take one. After all, we are not twenty, and who cares if the few years ahead offer diversion." He stops and looks at her solemnly.

Ruth smiles as she says lightly, "Dick, I think it would be fun to read Gertrude in the bedroom scene with you as Hamlet. By the way, do you think he was in love with his mother?"

"No, but I think I am falling in love with you. Don't laugh. And none of that unintelligible Gullah, please." She reaches for his hand.

"It's time for Sabbath vittles, Dick. Join us at our table for lunch. We girls will be happy to have a gentleman to break the monotony of female chatter."

The Sunny Acres dining room on Sunday is extended to the room adjacent as well as to the sun porch in order to accommodate visiting children and grandchildren. It is buffet day offering a variety of salads, entrées and desserts. As Richard and Ruth sign the book provided, they see Biddy punch her dinner partner and snicker a whisper in her ear. Ruth's eyes meet Biddy's boldly and flash her an "I heard what you said" message. Biddy responds by shrugging and lifting her appropriately large proboscis two inches higher. Having witnessed the wordless exchange between the two, Richard smiles broadly and says, "Excuse me, Miss Pritchett, but do I see a bee in your bonnet?" Biddy jerks off her wide-brimmed hat and searches for the bee in the cluster of yellow roses repeated in the skirt she is wearing. Ruth mumbles "naughty boy" but cannot resist a chuckle as they help themselves to the lavish display of salads.

The two amble across the extended dining room to seek out Ruth's usual table which is laid for six. There are startled looks on five faces as Ruth and Richard approach. Ruth offers to find a table to accommodate just two, but simultaneously the five swivel together to make room for another chair. They would not have missed this new addition for the world. What in the name of "all's well that ends well" is Ruth Smith doing with that eccentric Brit who has yet to recognize the Declaration of Independence? Will Ruth in her usual enigmatic way answer a question by quoting the bard—

"It's *much ado about nothing*"? Well, it's worth shoving plates and salads together to find out, and interrogation about intimacies is not above Sunny Acres, where nobody's business is everybody's business. After all, in a community or cuisine where the bland not the spice prevails, the tiniest morsel "sweetens the imagination."

It is Virginia who speaks first. Her reputation as "one of the characters" in Sunny Acres makes her seemingly innocent remarks funny and endearing. Unlike Biddy Pritchett, Virginia conveys neither malice nor attempt to stir up trouble. Virginia is just having fun, but her level of wit escapes those whose minds are not so keen. Ruth particularly enjoys her gentle barbs. After all, they are citizens under the skin, both having taught English. Of the two, Virginia is the scholar, and Ruth doesn't mind. Virginia wrote her dissertaion on the editions of Shakespeare's *Hamlet*. Textual differences are not Ruth's interest in the bard. Instead, she savors the language and its dramatic impact.

"Well, Richard, welcome to the Sappho Society," Virginia offers as a greeting.

Mary, who wears two hearing aids and misses three-fourths of any conversation, this time catches every syllable of Virginia's remark and laughs heartily. She welcomes the diversion of a male dinner guest. What she doesn't hear, she editorializes imaginatively, the result sometimes making lively conversation. Barbara and Betty exchange amused glances. They silently wonder what is so special about Richard Blair to Ruth Smith. Jane, who is a fairly new resident and who has attended every function and activity (including mistakenly signing the Count-Me-In sheet for the Gentlemen's Breakfast) in order to get to know her new community, asks innocently, "Who is Sappho? I haven't heard of that group before."

Richard, who stands as the waitress prepares an extra place at the table, grins as he addresses Jane. "Sappho was one of those ancient Greek ladies who lived on the Isle of Lesbos. She was the founder of the Republican Party and insisted that the president should have a woman for his running mate. You know—like Sarah Palin."

"Well, I like Sarah Palin. I think she has done a lot for this country. She's made people start thinking," Jane says.

"Sit down, Richard," Ruth orders. "You must have failed Greek History at Oxford." Turning to Jane, she adds, "And Jane, they are both pulling your leg. Besides, we don't discuss politics on the Lord's Day."

"Aw shucks, Ruth," Virginia laughs. "You spoil the fun. Democrats can't stand the heat. Welcome, Richard, and I hope you don't listen to all that liberal garbage."

"Of course not. I'm really a Fascist."

Jane, looking puzzled, eyes her new friends and wonders if she has stumbled into the wrong group. She has despaired so often that she didn't go to college. But she prides herself on her secretarial skills. Of course, that was the way she met her husband. He had left her a tidy sum before moving up the corporate ladder with his boss's blonde daughter who became his wife after a messy divorce. Jane decides to ask Biddy Pritchett about all of them. At the moment, however, all are interested in the man at the table. Rumor has it that Jane is a bit of a flirt. Sitting directly across from Richard, she directs her gray-blue eyes at him and speaks in that soft drawl with the elongated syllables characteristic of southern Georgia. "At last I'm going to have dinner with Mister Blair," she coos. "And I just love that English accent. Is it all right if I call you Richard? Everybody is so friendly here—like one big family. But I know the British are a little standoffish."

Richard smiles wickedly. "Oh, Janie, you must call me Dickie. And I just loveeeeeeee to hear you talk. You all's southern drawl warms the cockles of an old Brit's heart." Ruth raises her eyebrow, the stop signal for Richard to cut script.

"Come on, Richard," Ruth says. "Our cuisine has seemed appealing to your discriminating palate. Yams and fried chicken, you must admit, beats kidney stew any day."

"So long as we don't have grits for dessert. It's a damn shame what you Southerners have done to good corn. A pity you didn't stick with the bottle," Richard returns tartly.

"I don't understand, Dickie." Janie bats her eyes. "Don't you like grits? I just love them with country ham and red-eye gravy. They're so good they make you want to whip your grandpa." Richard looks puzzled. "You know I don't mean it. It's just an old Southern saying when we mean something is real good."

"Well, they make me want to kill my mother-in-law. That is if I had one."

"Is that one of your British sayings, Dickie?" Jane asks innocently.

"No, luv, I stole it from Shakespeare."

At that moment a loud crash galvanizes everyone's attention. Jasmine, a server on spring break from college, has just dropped Betty Keaton's tray. Jasmine is one of the recipients of the Sunny Acres Scholarship Fund. Betty is spared, but English peas roll down a gentleman's paunch and iced tea splatters his white slippers. Help comes in a hurry and minutes later the incident is forgotten as conversations resume on mundane things. Sunny Acres employees are always alert to emergencies and handle any crisis with the calm and proficiency of a paramedic.

Jane picks up the conversation. "I hear that our library is going to put a charge on overdue books. I just love to read. I turn my books in almost the next day after I check them out." She is trying to show the book lovers around the table that she shares a common interest.

"Well, overdue charges won't solve the problem with thieves," Ruth says. "The librarian tells me that even brand new books disappear as soon as they are put out. Can you imagine thieves among such an affluent Sunny Acres society?" Ruth thinks the subject of books will get conversation among this diverse group on an even keel. She forgets that Mary hears every third word and fills in the blanks and that Virginia always has a smart quip whether the dialogs be about the blandness of Cajun chicken or the merits of shopping at Wal-Mart over Publix regardless of the five percent discount at Publix on Wednesdays for seniors.

Mary's fork of spinach casserole is poised in the air. She has no intention of taking a bite until she questions Ruth. The one word that stands out for her is *thieves.*

"Ruth, what did they steal? Was it jewelry? Biddy Pritchett says she's lost one of her diamond earrings. She says each one is a carat and could be made into a ring."

"Don't worry, Mary," Virginia says soothingly. "Ruth is talking about books. If the librarian would tell me what the missing tome is, I could lay my finger on the culprit in an hour. I would bet that Richard Blair has all the first editions of Danielle Steele hidden behind the unabridged *Oxford English Dictionary.*" She leans toward Mary and raises her voice. "Mary, don't worry about Pritchett's missing earring. That pair is just rhinestones."

"And I just adore Danielle Steele," Jane adds. "But I see plenty of them in the library. And, Virginia, I don't believe Mr. Blair is a thief." She has forgotten to first-name him. She looks around and sees the smothered laughs. She knows she has made a faux pas but she does not understand what it is. Dick Blair is the only one not laughing. Eating in English fashion, he is about to lift with knife and fork a cut of roast beef to his mouth. Poor Jane's cheeks redden. Ruth decides to rescue her.

"Pay no attention to Virginia, Jane. She's so busy pulling people's legs that she doesn't have time to trail thieves. But as a matter of fact, you might find some books like Danielle Steele's in Dick's possession. You probably don't know Muriel Townshend who died here a few weeks ago. Dick knew her. She was a graduate of none other than the revered and sacred Oxford. She wrote dozens of romances. Know why? She found them easy to write, easy to sell, and an easy way to make healthy pounds, which she gave to charity. She was born in South Carolina but became Dame of the English Empire. Her chick lit made a greater contribution than the serious stuff I try to write embroidered with poetic allusions."

"Whose pulling a leg now, Ruth?" Virginia quizzes. "I suggest you leave your imagination in your laptop while you are eating Sunday dinner with friends."

Dick lays his silverware down carefully and lifts his napkin to brush a stray crumb from his shirt. "Ruth, for once," he smiles at her, "is telling the truth. I did not know Muriel was in Sunny Acres recovering from surgery. Ruth discovered her, but not her identity, until after she died."

"No, Dick, remember I told you that I found out the last day I read to her from what I considered cheap romances. I connected her to Hell Hole Swamp in South Carolina by an accent that slipped out. In fact, her pseudonym was Helen Hole. I really wanted to get to know her better. She had a fatal heart attack that night. I read her obit in the English *Times*. She was a journalist, a scholar, and a philanthropist."

Everyone stops eating, expecting more. Mary leans forward and adjusts her hearing aid.

"Well, there's not much to tell. Our conversation was cut off when she had to be taken to therapy. Anyway, she was amused to watch my amazement, and by then I think, or I hope, that she had found in me a kindred spirit. Both of us are daughters of the Low Country in South Carolina."

"Well, go on," Barbara urges.

"Her father was a white teacher who married a woman part Negro, Cherokee, and Caucasian. He came to the South recruited to be a math teacher and a principal of a high school. Of course, he brought his wife and little girl with him. Somehow the cat got out of the bag and his contract was not renewed. So they became a part of the Great Immigration north. Muriel was smart—brilliant—awarded a Rhodes Scholarship after college. Came back home only to die."

Richard adds, "She was a frequent visitor in my bookstore. She loved first editions. I did not know her background. In fact, I knew her as a respected journalist with a zeal for minorities getting an education." Dick's voice is slow and somber. "I wonder why she chose to come back," he mused.

"To make her peace with the past," Ruth says solemnly. Quiet falls upon the table. Jane has tears in her eyes. She rises suddenly from the table whispering, "Excuse me. I don't think I want dessert."

Ruth ponders as she watches Jane's retreating figure: *There's another story behind a door.*

SNOW OVER SUNNY ACRES

What northerners call anathema, southerners call god sent—all in reference to snow. In the middle of winter with no real holiday in sight, businesses and schools close. Children rush out, their hands raised heavenward to receive this white manna. If it accumulates, visions of snowmen and fist balls dance in their heads. Oldsters in Sunny Acres share memories of snow ice cream made with sugar and vanilla. One resident recalls the city paralyzed when the blessed event yielded fourteen inches thirty years ago. Another predicts, "It won't stick. Sun will be out tomorrow."

False prophet! Falling flakes mixed with sleet greet Sunny Acres the next morning. It is anathema indeed to the staff. More than four hundred souls to feed with no chef, no waitresses, no housekeepers. The media reports icy roads, numerous wrecks, cars stalled, power outages, and the mercury locked well below freezing for days. Ruth's Othello finds no grass on which to leave his calling card, ventures three steps in the white mass, slips, recovers, and heads for the safety of the patio. His concern is minor in comparison to the few staff who slip in over yet unmade snow ruts to prove their loyalty to Sunny Acres.

Not even the greatest writer can account for the miracle that happens. A regular cuisine is ready at noon, and an open buffet with sandwiches and hot soup provides the evening repast. What the residents observe in shocked admiration is every soul who has braved the storm is wearing an apron and cheerfully serving food. This group represents all divisions—the office, kitchen, housekeeping, and wellness staff or anyone else with willing hands and fast feet. Only the residents are excluded from the work force. Sunny Acres in white drapery is beautiful, but inside are warmth and well-fed residents enjoying nature's frolics from the safety of their abodes. There is no playing in the snow. Old feet slip too easily, and the younger feet are busy with a transition of a kitchen staff reduced to a handful of novices. A catastrophe has brought about camaraderie, and the irony is that the coldness of the outside has warmed the hearts of the staff as well as the residents. Even Biddy Pritchett praises the caretakers and declares that no other life care facility can boast such loving care. That coming from the chronic complainer is another miracle wrought by the silent snow falling like petals but making icy pyramids over Ruth's pansies. She has heard that ice can be warm and protective. As she and Othello stand on their patio, she hopes that soon she will see the resurrection of bright little violas, little variegated faces turning toward the sun. Othello yelps. Someone is at the front door.

CHESTER

"Oh, Chester, you shouldn't have bothered! Changing my closet light is not that important. Stop that, Othello! Do you know that you are barking at one of the most revered staff members at Sunny Acres? You should be ashamed of yourself as many times as Chester has been here."

The man at the door smiles. He stands around five feet four, a small man who works out daily answering the calls of residents, overseeing the renovation of apartments, supervising maintenance projects, helping people move, and doing any other needed job at Sunny Acres, because this man can do anything. He is always moving at a trot with that brown mop of hair flopping and bearing no definite cut from a barber. Although he always seems in a hurry, there is always time for a fast pat on a shoulder and a grin that stretches a ragged moustache across a lean face. *Hyper* is not strong enough as a description for Chester, who rushes from duties at Sunny Acres to volunteer at the Fire Department and the Sheriff's office or to respond to calls from the Security Team or the Ambulance Service. He should have a name that identifies him such as Chester the Good, because he spends every waking moment doing for others—from changing a light bulb in a closet at work to pulling a body from a lake as a Security Team member. He has been asked many times, "Chester, when do you stop? How do you relax?" He answers, "I relax when I'm helping people." He epitomizes the Golden Rule and the admonition "Love thy neighbor as thyself." But Chester the Good exceeds the commandment. For him, self is secondary to the needs of others.

"You look a little tired, Chester," Ruth tells him.

"Haven't been to bed since Saturday." Today is Tuesday.

"What have you been doing?"

"Hauling people to work who couldn't get here. Drove an ambulance to the hospital. Helped out in the kitchen. Maintenance had a contest on who could cook the best chili."

"Who won?"

"Me. First time I tried. Nothing to it. Brown a little beef, throw in cans of tomatoes and beans and chili powder." He grins. "Course I keep tasting. A spot of oregano, some more chili and red pepper, a dash of thyme and cumin. Nothing to it." By this time he has mounted a ladder and changed the light bulb and is heading for the door.

"Wait a minute, Chester. I'm writing a book about living in a life care community and I need to put in an interesting character on the staff. Would you tell me about yourself? Would you give me the time?"

He grins again. "Tell you what I'll do. When I get off work Thursday, I'll drop by. I can't tell you what time. Something always comes up."

"Don't you worry about the time. I'll be here with my notebook ready."

It is Thursday. Ruth hears the clock chime five. There is a knock at the door. Othello answers it with his little tenor voice.

"Come in, Chester. I've been looking forward to your coming. Sit down in that chair and rest those tired feet." Ruth points to a wingback chair with an ottoman. Othello continues his noisy greeting. Chester leans over and offers his hand. One sniff and Othello slumps at his feet ready for a pat on the head or a good scratching.

"My goodness, Chester, you have charisma with dogs. I rarely see Othello accept a guest so quickly."

"We loved animals. All kinds." He leans over and commences to scratch Othello's head. "We had pet

iguanas, lizards, and even snakes. I have a picture of
Mama with a boa constrictor around her neck."

"I love all kinds of animals, too, but snakes are not
one of them. Did you have some ordinary pets like
dogs?"

"Yes, Mama breeded Chihuahuas. It was a way of
supplementing her income. I remember at one time we
had one hundred and eleven Chihuahuas. She always
tried to get them good homes. Boy, could they make
a racket." Othello has rolled over and is thoroughly
enjoying getting his belly scratched. "Neighbors didn't
much like the noise."

"What did your father say about all those animals?"

He answers looking directly into Ruth's eyes. "I
never saw my dad. The army moved my mother and
two brothers into a safe house down here. I was born
three months later. My dad was a mean man. My mama
found out he had six other wives strung across the
states. The army finally nailed him. Sent him to Fort
Leavenworth. Was only forty-six when he died."

"Chester, how in the world did your mother support
three children?"

"Five children. She had two by her first marriage.
She worked two jobs each day. I got siblings everywhere.
Went up to New York a few years back and met three of
my half brothers." He chuckles. "Another could turn
up any day. My dad had twenty-one children in all."
He laughs as though siring that many children is as
ordinary as siring two or three.

"Well, you children didn't have much supervision with your mom working all the time."

"You are right about that. We had us a good time. We'd put on our thickest clothes and shoot each other with our BB guns. One thing we loved to do was to go to the airport and shoot out lights with rubber bands and then hide and watch a worker put in new bulbs."

"For heaven's sake! Didn't you think about causing a plane crash?"

"Oh, we didn't do it near the runways."

"Did you ever get arrested?"

"No, but the Sherriff picked us up one night. Wanted to know why we were out on the street so late. He drove us around until my mama got off work and then took us to her. He was a good old guy. He knew boys will be boys. He also knew my mama and how hard she worked."

"Well, how about your school work. What kind of grades did you make?"

"I was a "B" student. Always had trouble with reading. Something affected my memory, too. You know I can't remember two minutes later what people tell me in the hall. Everybody said I'd never amount to anything. See, I dropped out of school three months before I could graduate. Don't even have a GED. Got married at eighteen. That was a bad mistake."

"Why did you drop out? You were so close to graduation."

"Things were pretty bad at home. Mama away working all the time. We had a real bad older sister. Me and my brothers use to jump out the window to get away from her and we lived upstairs."

"What happened then?"

"I started helping, doing carpenter work. I found out I could duplicate anything I saw. See that chair over there? I could build that chair. No good at reading directions. Then I started working at the Sherriff's office. Started messing around with equipment like running projectors. I found out I could make anything run. Somehow I learned along the way that I was happiest when I was helping people. So I've been doing what makes me happy ever since. And you know. The Golden Rule. Do unto others like you would have them do to you."

"Go to church, Chester?"

"Somebody asks me that I tell them I'm in church every day helping others and I pray all the time."

Ruth smiles. "And *loving your neighbor as yourself.* I think you love your neighbor better than yourself. What you have is a degree in human love and kindness."

He pulls from his billfold an identification card that certifies him as an emergency respondent. He smiles broadly. "I took the course and missed only three questions on the final hundred-question test."

"But you said you can't read."

"Oh, it was multiple choice. Beside, toward the end I was teaching the class."

"Chester, I am overwhelmed. What about your home life?"

"My wife and I divorced after the children grew up. But Cindy and I have been together eleven years. Believe it or not I met her at Lowe's. She is a nurse and with the army. She has twenty-six names behind her name. She does highly classified work with the army, but we know where each other is every minute or how to get in touch with each other. Last year she was on assignment in Kuwait. She called the house. I had just left. She called Sunny Acres. Hadn't arrived. Called the Sherriff. Just left. She finally caught up with me. Oh, by the way. She is a volunteer with the Sherriff's Department also." At that point his phone rings. It is Cindy. She is still at work. Ruth speaks to her briefly and expresses a desire to meet her.

Then Ruth asks Chester, "What about all this recognition you get? Employee of the month five times. Didn't you get some community service award in Washington?"

"Yep! And I got tapped on the shoulder by a CIA for being in restricted areas. One time it was because I was waving at the White House. Each time I gave them five types of identification. The last time a CIA officer put me on the metro to go to my hotel where I would be safe and where Cindy could keep me out of trouble." They both laugh. Othello barks and wags his tail to show that he, too, feels it is funny.

"And your children, Chester?"

"We each have two. All of them out of school and doing well. One big, happy family. Cindy and I have something special going. We know when to talk and when not to. It's that kind of relationship. She's the best thing that ever happened to me." The tone is serious but the face still smiles.

"Chester, that is exactly what she said to me on the phone about you. You know, your life would make a best seller. Why don't you write it?"

"Miss Smith, you forget that I have a literacy problem. Anyway, I have too much to do. Remember what makes me happy?"

"Yes, shooting out lights and playing soldier with your BB guns." Ruth and he laugh together as he rises. "Gotta go. Cindy will be getting off work about now."

BIRCHES

Ruth sits on her patio reviewing the past seasons. Her mind sweeps through pallets of color, breaths of spring, the ripening of Georgia peaches, the flaming dress of fall. It is winter now but not a typical southern winter. The wind pierces the fleece of her jacket, and Othello snuggles even closer. Snow has been falling for two days, wrapping Sunny Acres in white, a monotony interrupted with an occasional crash of black limbs. Joseph and Nan Lawrence are dead. A road winding to their mountain cabin slid their Toyota downward to instant death. Ruth would like to think that they were surrounded by tall birches left unscathed and standing sentinel. She thinks to herself: *What shall I say at the Memorial Service this afternoon as I speak to the residents of Sunny Acres locked in by winter but bonded like a family who have assembled to remember?*

How vividly she remembers. A couple holding hands after sixty-seven years together, their only wish to share the ending. Theirs—a storybook story, not a myth, a love palpable in the way they retold their past spun in a romance woven with humor. Should there be mourning since their wish had been granted? No, she decided, the grief should be for those deprived of such love—those upon whom the gods had not smiled to confer it. Even so, a tear slips down her cheek.

There is not an empty chair in the Georgia Room, where the residents gather for the service. A gold cross centers the stage flanked by urns of holly, which grows by their cottage. The berries are Christmas red. Ruth rises to give the last memorial as Samuel Barber's "Adagio for Strings" begins. At the end of her eulogy, she offers this closing:

Once upon a time there were two birches.
They were planted on the same day.
One day in the spring of the year
They had grown so tall that they touched.
Through the years their leaves
Caressed—
Each year they grew stronger
And closer.
They withstood storm, rain and wind.
Today they still stand
Perhaps wearing snow, as their branches rise to eternity.

Barber plays on and Ruth walks to the door, momentarily followed by a silent group.

In the privacy of her home, Ruth weeps. There is a gentle tap on the door. Ruth dries her eyes and bids the caller entrance. It is Richard. He gathers her in his arms and holds her close. "It was the most beautiful eulogy I have ever heard. I only wish the Lawrences could have heard it."

"How do you know that they didn't?" she says softly.

LOBSTER TIME

Sunny Acres has a new chef. Previous to his appearance, there have been complaints about the dining room ranging from polite disgruntlement to lionized roars. The soup is cold. The soup is too hot. It has burned ulcers in several mouths. The soup is too spicy. It irritates stomachs with irritable bowel syndrome. The soup is bland—tasteless. With eyes closed, one cannot tell whether it is cream of asparagus or potato. Prime rib is tough. Specially ordered, it comes bloody or charred. Cream congeals when it is stirred into coffee served much too cold. And to make the situation worse, long before a meal is finished, the staff begins clearing tables and setting out accoutrements for the next meal, an act that so enraged one resident that he choked on a last bite of pecan pie and had to be rushed to the emergency room, where an overworked intern found no trace of pie or pecan in the resident's windpipe. Into this environment comes a brand new chef who is expected to turn Sunny Acres dining overnight into a grand cuisine.

The residents are excited. Anne Byrd doffs her overalls, gentlemen don ties and coats reserved for church, and five ladies come in evening dress with one wearing a rhinestone tiara glittering enough to authenticate real diamonds. Biddy Pritchett, determined to outshine the flash in her neighbor's crown, has come in a Chinese multicolored caftan with a string of sparkling lights around her neck. After all, it is just three weeks before Christmas and the sun porch is aglow with the season's miniature trains, animals, and villages over which a rotund St. Nick winks in Yuletide cheer. Chester's annual display is the joy of residents and visitors. The dining room décor repeats the coming holiday with a massive tree loaded with ribboned presents and symmetrically decorated in bells and angels luminous in a thousand lights. A bulletin has been posted and copies placed in mailboxes to prepare everyone for this festive evening when new Chef Pierre will show his stuff.

The rumor mill has been in operation ever since the announcement. Pros and cons about animal cruelty have been debated in humanitarian huddles over cocktails on drink-free Thursday and in spirited discussions at Vespers as to what is the best method to cook a live lobster that will insure the most painless demise without sacrificing the taste. Dr. Goldstein, who claims to have a Ph.D. in ichthyology, posted in the weekly newsletter plans for a free lecture on lobster anatomy prior to the feast. The sun porch is packed with pre-feasters. Dr. Goldstein begins her erudite dissertation by explaining that the lobster's brain is the size of that of a grasshopper, so the scientific consensus is that a lobster feels no pain. However, Chef Pierre has assured her that prior to boiling, a lobster will be numbed by a short trip to the freezer. Chef Pierre, our Ph.D., has a great sense of humor. He asks, "Why should a lobster never walk into a kitchen? Answer: Because it is a trap that will finally end him up in the bedroom or parlor." Nobody laughs. Chef Pierre's wit is too subtle. Perhaps he should confine his jokes to the kitchen. One resident raises her hand. There is an educated smirk on her face.

"Dr. Goldstein, I notice that Chef Pierre refers to lobsters as male. I am a feminist and resent excluding the female gender even if the subject is lobsters."

"Oh, I agree. Chef Pierre knows now that they can be male or female. I had a session with him this afternoon. In fact, the shipment from Maine must have split the sexes—half and half. We examined a random sample. Half and half."

"Something fishy about that," quips Richard Blair, whose puns often fall on deaf ears. This remark, however, brings forth peals of laughter. "How could you tell?"

"Easy. The female has a wider tail that holds the sperm. And guess what. It takes as long as ten months for the babies to hatch depending on the temperature of the water. Longer than human babies."

"I bet a lot of them never get born. I can't imagine fisherman taking special regard for pregnant mothers." This again from the feminist.

"You're wrong about that." Richard has just returned from a trip to Nova Scotia. "In Nova Scotia the license for fishing lobsters costs six-hundred thousand dollars." The room heaves surprise and denial. "Of course, the license is for a lifetime. It can be revoked if the regulators discover too many berried lobsters."

"Buried in what, pray tell?" the feminist asks.

"B-e-r-r-i-e-d," spells Dr. Goldstein, who looks down her nose at such ignorance. "That is the term for pregnant lobsters. And by the way, a female lobster is called a hen when she weighs one pound. This is the only species which gets reward for gaining weight."

"Aren't there other ways to lessen the strictures of death? I just don't want to think about death pangs as I douse a clump of dead lobster in drawn butter."

"Oh, yes," explains Dr. Goldstein. "Some have been administered mild anesthesia. Some have been hypnotized by standing them on their heads. You can measure the length of time before death by counting the twitches once they are placed in the boiling water."

"Amanda," says Biddy Pritchett, "you have ruined my dinner. I'm going to order vegetables." She turns off her winking necklace and stomps out onto the sun porch.

"Biddy, just remember that every crunch of your lettuce is a squeal. At least the lobster is dead." Dr. Goldstein's parting thrust is unheard.

Ruth sits at the table with two old friends: Michael, an ophthalmologist, and his wife, Sybl. They are parents of former students. Richard makes the fourth and Evalyn completes the quintet. She would read more books than Ruth, if she dropped four committees and cancelled three trips. Ruth and Richard have entertained them with Dr. Goldstein's lecture, which two of them have missed. They have all been paper bibbed and now await the *piece de resistance*. At that moment a trio of choristers wearing thigh-length skirts in earth colors has entered the dining room singing: "All things bright and beautiful, all creatures great and small, all things wise and wonderful, the great God loves them all." They are bearing placards proclaiming, "PROTECT OUR MARINE LIFE; DON'T EAT THEM!" Each protester is wearing a mask, one painted with the face of a shrimp, one with a clam and one with a lobster. Sibyl giggles. "I knew this was going to happen. Those three are allergic to shellfish." Chef Pierre, whose smiling face has metamorphosed into perplexity close to alarm, stands transfixed, clutching a platter of steaming lobsters. Being new, he is unfamiliar with Sunny Acres humor. Adding still more to his confusion, the singers approach him and drop a bouquet of fresh vegetables at his feet before sidling off into the pantry. A resonant baritone from one of the tables booms, "The show is over. Bring on the vittles!" General applause follows. Michael leans over so that Ruth can hear and asks: "Is this Sunny Acres or vaudeville?"

"Neither," replies Ruth. "This is Geriatrics Revival—oldsters having a good time, not thinking about the recent fate of three hundred lobsters, or their own for that matter. A good thing to make merry at our age, yes?" Michael turns abruptly in response to a tweak on the bow of his bib. It is Iris, a patient of his.

"Excuse me, Mike. That dumb husband of mine has just squirted lobster juice in my eye. Could you take a look?"

"Not to worry, Iris." He stands and raises her eyelid. "A little saline solution might burn but would be good for your eye."

"Even though I had cataract surgery yesterday?"

Somebody at the next table calls, "Poor timing, Iris, to consult your ophthalmologist. Sit down. Here comes the chef with our lobster." Iris gives him a balled fist as she makes her way back to her husband.

It is time for Richard to engage in a little poetry. Kipling is one of his favorite writers.

> *Women, women! Lean or fat*
> *The face of an angel*
> *And the soul of a cat.*

"Behave yourself," Ruth whispers.

Soon an odd silence pervades the dining room—broken only by the sound of crushing shells and slurps as the residents of Sunny Acres taste the succulent essence from the amputated claws. Then a low rumble rises much like the soup complaints of yore. "I never heard of having lobster without corn on the cob."

"Down in Charleston they always serve lobster with grits."

"Could you tell whether yours was male or female?"

"I never saw butter like this."

"That's what drawn butter is, darling."

"I just nicked my finger. Anyone got a Band-Aid?"

"I know my lobster didn't weigh a pound. My hen turned out to be a biddy."

"Did you call me?" The voice belongs to Biddy Pritchett. She has just sucked the last lobster claw belonging to her dinner partner who has always been a light eater.

OUR REVELS NOW ARE ENDED

It is spring again. In pensive mood Ruth Smith sits with her PC in her lap and contemplates the past twelve months. Just a year ago she wrote the opening of *Sunny Acres,* not knowing where it was going, but obeying that itching to take up pen once more, to record remembrances of things past and to anticipate the future—the happy days and those not so happy. And now she is drawn once more to the laptop. "I must find an ending," she whispers to herself. "Where did I begin this tale?" She clicks on the *Sunny Acres* icon she finds and reads the opening. She spies on George Clark grieving for his lost Molly. She sees Richard Blair, the Englishman and lover of books, trying to console him in the tactful way of the Brits, and overhears Biddy

Pritchett rumoring to Anna Faulk that George is already "carrying on" with Betty Keaton though poor Molly is "not even cold in her grave." She reaches down to pat Othello. "What a year it has been, honey bunch! You are a year older and I am close to ending *Sunny Acres.*"

She turns again to the text before her and smiles as she fills in the future. Biddy Pritchett's rumors about Ruth and Richard have some truth in them. He has become very significant in her life. And yesterday George Clark and Betty Keaton were married in a simple ceremony using nature as their church. Ruth reaches for the picture Richard took and gazes at the beautiful scene. George and Betty stand in front of the tulip garden, edging the lake. What a glorious mass of red, orange, yellow and white in the pink cloud of blossoms in the Yoshino cherry trees! Betty is wearing a simple mauve suit with an orchid on her jacket. George wears a light blue business suit with a white rose in his button hole. Behind them is the Elizabeth Marie Meyer Memorial Garden, to honor the wife of Hans, both natives of Holland. Susie and Jerry Saul, who initiated the planting of tulips, thought that springtime flowers from Elizabeth's native land were a way to remember an outstanding woman, brave enough to shield Jews from the Nazis during the Holocaust. Somber and sacred. The stillness of the lake with a springtime altar of flowers, a couple holding hands, and a woman whose name is written in beauty—"there is no holier spot of ground."

Now here comes Anne. Ruth recognizes the special knock at her door. Anne is holding a camel in her arms and a paper with a drawing in her hands. Ruth does not understand the significance of the camel but she knows what is on the paper. It is the latest creation of Anne's tabby cat, Cookie Dough, who, by pushing her food with her paw sometimes makes a discernible pattern that Anne believes is actually art. Anne has validated the ability of cats to paint by finding a book on that subject. Now it seems that she has added to her scholarship in bees and bats information about the camel. In addition, this morning Anne is sporting a new haircut that is just inches away from being a buzz cut. It may be that she has added to her menagerie a porcupine, hence the blonde tresses sticking straight up. A stranger might think that here is a woman literally scared to death. Not so. Anne Byrd is fearless and loving to both man and beast, the only exception being anyone registered a democrat. Ruth smiles as she waits to be enlightened on the merits of a dromedary.

"Pretty early, Anne, to have walked a mile." Ruth waits for her to catch the allusion to the forties ad for a cigarette: *I'd walk a mile for a camel.*

"Whatcha mean? I just...." A smile broadens her face. "Oh, you mean the camel. I just thought you needed to include a little valuable information about my latest pet. And I brought Cookie Dough's latest art." She holds up a single sheet of paper. "Don't you think it looks like Van Gogh's *Sunflowers?*"

"Well, indeed, it looks like a sunflower—very like a sunflower." Ruth laughs as she mimics Polonius in *Hamlet*. She thinks, *Anne won't catch this.* But how wrong Ruth is.

"Oh, stop that Shakespeare stuff. Anyway, he's dead and gone. I bet you didn't know that the camel was one of the first animals to be created and he's still around. And talk about art. Look at his feet. Perfectly designed for the sandy deserts of the Middle East." She fingers the foot. Her voice is reverent as though she is in church.

"One of God's creations." Ruth, too, is serious now.

"I have another imaginary pet. Been doing this as a child. I read about him and think how beautifully and thoughtfully he is made. It's like looking at a stained glass window, isn't it." They both smile and Anne, holding the hump to her breast, says, "See you at dinner. And yes, I have included Richard. Got a table for five."

Ruth's fingers begin typing. What a wonderful asset to Sunny Acres. A comedian with a heart as warm as those of the animals, stray and imaginary, that she loves—a heart which knows the value of laughter, particularly in a life care community.

The telephone rings. "Darn, I'll never finish *Sunny Acres* at this rate." Ruth lifts the phone and reads the caller ID. Billy Watkins. The mystery man in overalls on weekdays and in Armani on Sundays. "Hello."

"This is Billy. You know. Flush's papa. I hope you're not busy."

"Not too busy to talk to you. How is Flush?"

"Not good. I just had to put him to sleep."

"Oh, Billy!

"Couldn't let him suffer. I've seen too much of that."

"Billy, I'm putting on a pot of coffee. If you want something stronger, I can manage that, too."

"Are you sure?"

"I'm certain."

Ruth opens the screen door and stands on the patio waiting for Billy. In just a moment he appears. He wears the pants to his Sunday suit with a white dress shirt opened at the collar. The gray head is bowed as though he must focus on his feet to avoid stumbling. Ruth meets him halfway down the cobblestones. He stops and faces her. His face is set, waxen; his eyes, marbled. Ruth extends her hand. Now the lips move into a childish primp, though no tears fall. She grasps his right hand and sheathes it in hers. Walking backward, she draws him into her living room. Othello neither barks nor wags his tail. She guides Billy to the convenient wingback. From that vantage point he can survey the portraits of her former pets. She wishes she had seated him elsewhere. His sunken brown eyes seem drawn to them like a magnet. At last he speaks, slowly, without inflection—like a child reading from a first grade primer. "Tell me about the first one on the left second row."

"Her name was Betsy. She never weighed more than four pounds. She is the only one of my long-coat Chihuahuas who is not named for a Shakespearean character. Her name when she came to me from the kennel, her home for two years, was Bitsy. Not to traumatize her by a name change, I simply changed the vowel. Elizabeth, the great Shakespeare's queen. Betsy was too little to have babies. That was the only reason the breeder agreed to sell her. Beautiful blonde, isn't she?"

"Mary Grace, my wife, couldn't have babies either. Then William came at fifty-five. Her psychosis. William was very real to her. A grown man away at school. She would buy cashmere sweaters for him, which I gave to the Salvation Army. She baked his favorite cake. Sent him money on his birthday. She wondered why he didn't come home. Then one day she shot and killed the new postman, angry that he, William, was delivering mail and not finishing his degree. Now she has forgotten what she did. Always asks about him when I go to see her. She will miss Flush. Loved dogs. Hated her name. Nothing sacred about a name Mary Grace belonging to a woman who couldn't have children." Silence. Ruth finally finds her voice.

"Would you like something? Coffee? A drink?"

"No, nothing. Thought maybe I'd ask a favor. When I get Flush's ashes, I'd kinda like to scatter them around our favorite walks. Thought maybe you would care to walk with me. You and Othello. Kinda crazy asking you being I've been so distant. Know you love dogs. Know you like poetry. Maybe you could quote a few lines for Flush." He smiles now. "I guess when it comes to animals, I'm just what you would call a sentimental slop. Anyway—Named for Mrs. Browning's dog. You the only one caught it. Mary Grace loved Mrs. Browning."

"*How do I love thee? Let me count the ways.*" Ruth quotes quietly.

Billy pulls himself to his feet.

"I'll call you."

"Don't go, Billy."

"You understand," he says softly.

"I do." She slides the screen door open and watches him go down the walk. Othello follows him, and Billy reaches down to pat his ears. He turns back momentarily.

"Thanks."

Ruth closes the laptop. She can't write now. Instead, she goes to the bathroom, brushes her hair, and freshens her lipstick.

The dining room at lunch is still. A few diners are lingering over dessert. Alicia, the hostess, directs Ruth to a table. Ruth needs that smile that Alicia always wears. And somehow there is both comfort and stability in her unvarying attire. The tailored jacket over slacks always looks professional. She has a round face with flawless skin. Her light brown hair is smooth on her head and falls into a shoulder-length ponytail lightly curled. She has unwavering, attentive eyes as she listens to diners. Always eager for a bit of chat and even tolerant of complaints, Alicia is a sunny part of Sunny Acres—even in the darkness of a power failure—and adds such cheer to the dining room with her beautiful and artistic flower arrangements. Perhaps she reads distress on Ruth's face. Placing a glass of water down without lemon (she has the capacity not only to know the name of all the residents but also to remember their preferences), she lingers at the table.

"Alicia, tell me something funny that has happened at Sunny Acres."

Alicia turns her head in contemplation of the past and answers, "Let me see. Well, a couple of weeks ago there was a birthday party going in the private dining room. They had finished their dinner and it was time to bring in the cake. One of the waitresses holding a beautifully decorated chocolate cake headed the procession to sing 'Happy Birthday.' Just before we got to the door of the dining room, the cake slipped from her fingers. It landed on the floor in a brown mush of candles, chocolate frosting, yellow cake, and broken china."

"What in the world did you do?"

"I raced to my car and headed for Publix. Fifteen minutes later I was back with chocolate cake and candles. We were all ready to sing 'Happy Birthday.'"

"Did the diners find out?"

"No. The server refilled their wine glasses and they never noticed the time."

"And you, Alicia? No traffic tickets. No running and falling?

"No. But I had to be extra careful. I had bought the last chocolate cake the grocery store had."

"By this time the split pea soup and mandarin side salad have arrived. Alicia drifts away and Ruth raises her soup spoon. It is good to laugh. She wonders if Billy Watkins will ever laugh again. She knows there is no use to question why. To call it unfair—a psychotic wife and now the loss of his companion. "Life," she mumbles to herself. At this point Alicia wanders over to the table.

"Miss Smith, I just thought of the craziest thing. It happened a number of years ago. The chef and I were presenting our signature dessert in the assisted living dining room. I don't even remember what it was. What I do remember is that we had put it in the center of a white draped table and surrounded it with sparklers."

"Don't tell me."

"Yep, there was an explosion and the whole table flamed. It was a mad sight with half a dozen of us trying to snuff out the flames with anything handy. Our wise chef had a fire extinguisher and saved the day. That ended demonstrations of our signature dessert."

"Were the residents frightened?"

"Actually I think some of them thought the whole thing had been planned."

"You've got to be kidding, Alicia."

"Word of honor. Worse things have happened at Sunny Acres and residents never knew."

"You're right about that, Alicia."

Alicia leans over, covers one side of her face and whispers, "Mrs. Brodsky's incident with the black instructor during the blackout everybody knows about. I feel really sorry for her. She is still so embarrassed that she seldom eats in the dining room. When she does, she is usually alone. She's really a very nice person. Too bad that had to happen."

"I know. What she called the policeman slipped out. Racial prejudice runs deep. Most people would deny it. It's not politically correct to be a racist. Yet one of our most popular news anchors told our President on public television that people hated him. *Hate* is such a strong word. You know, Alicia, I've been thinking lately. Even though we have here at Sunny Acres such a warm family-like relationship, we still have pariahs— people like Carmen Brodsky, and Billy Watkins and even Biddy Pritchett. They are loners. There are some here that nobody wants to share a meal with. We need to do something about them."

"I agree. I think the new experiment with the sign-up table to get to know other people is a good idea. Here comes Amy. Our new Employee of the Month." Amy is a tall blonde waitress who, though she has not been at Sunny Acres long, has endeared herself to everyone whom she serves. She says she loves to make people smile and appears to be successful in achieving just that.

"Hi, Miss Smith. I'm looking forward to going back to school in the fall to get my degree. Thanks to the Sunny Acres Scholarship fund, I'm going to be able to manage it." She smiles and adds, "I know. I wouldn't dare not to, even if I didn't want to because you would be on my case every day. I was talking to Caramel—you know, the beautician. She's getting her degree in English in December. She says she loves Shakespeare."

Ruth laughs, remembering Caramel quoting Lady Macbeth when she spilled drops of hair dye on Biddy's pants. "She's a smart girl, our Caramel. I'm proud of her and proud of our scholarship that has made it easier for her."

"We're going to give her a party, and guess what we're going to eat."

"Caramel cake, of course."

"You got it, Miss Smith."

As Alicia and Amy wander off toward the kitchen, Ruth walks over to check her mail. Richard is standing nearby tossing unwanted advertisements into the junk receptacle. He looks around to scan the hall and plants a kiss on Ruth's cheek. She swerves around quickly and busies herself at her mailbox.

"What's for dinner, love?"

"Oh, Richard, I know I said I'd cook, but I just don't feel like it. Something very sad has happened."

"Tell me about it."

"Not here. I might cry. Let's go take Othello for a walk."

The two walk together toward the elevator. He makes no effort to question her further. Once they arrive at Ruth's door, Richard waits while she closes it. He pats friendly Othello, who gives Richard his usual high soprano greeting.

Ruth reaches over and draws a tissue from a box on her desk. She knows now that she will not be able to restrain her tears, and it is good that she will have a shoulder to cry on. "Billy Watkins has had to put Flush to sleep." She drops into a chair and dabs her eyes.

"How do you know? The man talks to nobody."

"He came to see me. Oh, Dick. What a horrible tragedy. I don't mean just losing Flush. It's his whole life. I just can't go into it right now. Anyway, he wants Othello and me to walk with him when he scatters Flush's ashes."

Richard leans over and puts his arm around her. He says gently, "He couldn't have asked a better person."

"I was trying to finish up *Sunny Acres* when he called and came over. Oh, my! I wonder if I saved what I was writing." She turns to the laptop and tries to bring up her screen. But despite her best efforts, it remains dark.

"What's happened, Richard?"

"Shut it down and try once more." Ruth clasps her hands and watches the screen. Still it remains dark. Suddenly, hope lightens her eyes.

"The memory stick. Everything is on the memory stick." She turns quickly to her desk. Her trembling fingers pull open the second drawer on the left. Her hand searches frantically. Then she dumps all the contents on the desk. Staples. Scotch tape. A hole puncher. Paper clips. A miniature Rudolph, the red-nosed reindeer with jingle bells around his neck. No memory stick. "I have no hard copy, Richard. I think somebody has stolen my memory stick— somebody who does not want *Sunny Acres* to be published."

"That's complete nonsense, my dear. Everyone at Sunny Acres is looking forward to its coming out this year. You have hidden the memory stick somewhere else. You know how you are always losing things."

"No, Dick. Not this time. I keep it in one place so that when my editor, Peggy, comes around, she can double check to see that the latest revision has been saved."

"Who would want to destroy *Sunny Acres?*"

"I don't know. Although it's a work of fiction, some of my characters bear a strong resemblance to real people. Some people might take offense."

"But who?

"Dick, I have no idea. In the words of Shakespeare, *My project was to please.* I had no intent to offend anyone. I just wanted to share with the world the sorrow and joy behind a few doors in Sunny Acres." Tears gather in her eyes as she whispers, "I wasted a whole year."

"Not entirely." He puts his arms around her. "Once more a Brit surrenders." He lifts her left hand and slips a small diamond on her third finger. His voice is slow as he whispers Prospero's words: *"Let your indulgence set me free."*